The Man At The
Rialto Bridge

Also by Janet Simcic

THE MAN AT THE CAFFE' FARNESE, a novel

AN AMERICAN CHICK'S GUIDE TO ITALY,
a work of non-fiction

REVIEWS

Janet Simcic's women's fiction novel, *The Man at the Rialto Bridge,* is a mix of family conundrum, spy thriller, and pure romance across generations. She has managed to create characters which inspire, and sometimes annoy a reader. The annoyance part works to build tension, and the result is a wonderful story, an easy to read page-turner. As a male who reads thrillers, and a writer who writes them, I found this a compelling read with insights I could learn from. You won't be disappointed with *The Man at the Rialto Bridge.*

DSKane, Amazon Bestselling Author of the *Spies Lie Series.*

In the manner of the classic mystery writers, Janet Simcic takes the tightly enclosed world of a cruise ship and gives you mystery, intrigue, overwhelming emotion, and a bit of romance. And again, because this is Simcic, you get her outstanding knowledge of Italy and the cruise world (right down to the drink of the day) and a highly satisfactory conclusion to the mystery and to the family dynamics that fuel this, her second 'Man at…' book. You'll want to read, and travel to Italy with Janet Simcic.

Brenda Barrie
Author of:

An Unorthodox Romance
The Rabbi's Husband
The Binding

The Man At The Rialto Bridge

Janet Simcic

GRAY MATTER IMPRINT EDITION

Published by Gray Matter Imprints, division of Gray Matter Consultants
LLC, P.O. Box 50278 Irvine, CA 92619

Printed in the United States of America

Publisher's Note: This novel is a work of fiction. The names, characters,
organizations, places and incidents are either the product of the author's
imagination or, as in the case of places in Europe, are used fictitiously,
and any resemblance to actual persons (living or dead), events or locales is
entirely coincidental.
ISBN: 0986285307
ISBN 13: 9780986285301

Dedication

To my wonderful husband, Bill, who puts up with my
endless hours on the computer, being banished to his man
cave for hours while my critique group meets,
And for his love!

Table of Contents

Mediterranean Cruise
Day One – Port Of Rome
Olivia
Boarding Area

*I*t had been exactly two hundred sixty-four days since my ex-husband had looked into my eyes and said, "I'm sorry. I don't love you as I should…as you deserve."

And what did that mean? You either love someone or you don't. But it still smarted. Fifteen years of marriage gone, as though it never happened. I glanced at my left hand, finally free of the wedding band I'd kept on all this time to protect myself…from questions or any man maybe taking a look. Yesterday, I'd taken the wedding band to one of those "we'll buy your gold guys" and received $3,000 in compensation for all those years.

From the moment I handed over the ring, I experienced a deep despair, which explained how desperate things had to be for me, single again, to spend twelve days on a European cruise with my older sister and my mother, the queen of dysfunction. Being on a ship with them was bad enough, but since childhood I'd gotten car sick, sea sick, and rollercoaster-ride sick. Twelve gruesome days with family I didn't like right now. I could only hope everything I'd heard about stabilizers on the new mega ships was true.

I had a secret, though. Otherwise I'd have never caved in to this trip. Many years of research had finally paid off. I reached into my pants pocket and fingered the photo.

Leaning on the rail waiting for the sail-away, the strains of *Arrivederci, Roma* mournfully being played by a calypso band, I noted a delicious white-uniformed officer sidle alongside my sister, Ashley. He nodded.

Ashley, showing even white teeth, thanks to recent da Vinci veneers, flashed him a Kodak smile.

Mom sidled right next to Ashley. "Ash," she said through her teeth, "you've barely put the last shovel of dirt on your husband's casket."

I eased away from the family tension at the rail. From the corner of my eye, I spotted a shock of dark hair. I turned to get a better look. He was tall, slim but not too slim, his face solemn, a straight nose with a slight flair at the nostrils, deep brown eyes fringed with black lashes, and cropped curly dark brown hair with no hint of gray.

He stared at the sea as though he didn't see it. In his hand, he held a glass of something blue in his hand. Probably the drink of the day. A Rolex, just like the one my ex had worn, adorned his wrist. I wanted to see this man smile.

Feeling brave, I circled to the other side of him and found a free space on the railing.

"Isn't the sea beautiful?" *Did I really say that?*

He turned as though in slow motion and looked at me. I wanted to slip into those espresso eyes and stay there. He hesitated; but in that pause, I felt him assessing me. It felt good to have a man really look at me after being dumped by a cheating husband.

I decided to assess right back, noting his untucked cream dress shirt, linen slacks that cupped his thighs and backside in the breeze. He'd topped the shirt with a blue blazer, and his feet were bare in expensive Italian loafers.

I switched the drink I'd been nursing and offered him my right hand.

"Hi. My name is Olivia Hillman."

"Nice to meet you, Olivia. I like that name. I'm Tony."

I'd had a bad track record with men. Two of them had left huge holes in my heart. But this one sent a spark through me, something I'd not experienced in years.

"So are you traveling alone?" He reached over and removed my sunglasses.

I backed away, startled.

"Sorry," he said. "I have a thing about seeing someone's eyes when I'm talking to them. You know, that old thing about the eyes being the something or other to the soul." He smiled, his teeth white and even, his lips, well, kissable.

"Not a problem. Um, I'm traveling with my mom and sister."

I had the feeling he was reading me again. Almost like he had a scanner that reached into my heart for some secret I was holding.

"Oliviaaa!"

"I think someone's looking for you," Tony said.

My teeth clenched. "That would be my sister."

"I see you're not married, although it looks like a ring once circled this finger," he said, holding my hand. I felt a tingling in my stomach.

"Yes. Single again," I muttered, looking down. "Maybe I'll see you later."

"I'm counting on that, Olivia." He touched my arm, donned his sunglasses and walked away, stopped to look back, lowered his glasses and winked.

"No, no, no," I told myself. Not ready for a man in my life yet.

"Olivia, you didn't introduce us," Ashley said.

"I'm sure we'll run into him again," I muttered, trying to keep sarcasm from my voice.

"I want to meet our butler," Ashley said.

Butler? I trotted behind my sister, the seasoned cruiser, as she glided across the deck to an elevator, my frail mom, clutching her arm, almost running to keep up.

Ashley, the epitome of perfection...smart, tall, willowy, blond...ash blond, actually...with sapphire eyes and pouty lips (no doubt enhanced by a Restylane injection or two in the last few years) had bossed me all my life. I thought of her as my personal velvet steamroller.

"Hurry up, gals. The elevator's here."

The art deco doors opened into a mirrored elevator with plush red velvet seats. It was a bit over the top for my taste. More over-the-top Victorian than elegant.

Once inside, Ashley slid her room key into a slot marked 'private,' next to a bronze plate reading 'Garden Villa.' The door hummed shut, and up we went. When the elevator doors popped open, I thought there had been a huge mistake. We were at the top of the ship, alone and far away from the crowds below. It felt like a tropical paradise.

A gentleman introduced himself. "Good day. I'm Christopher, your butler for the voyage. Welcome to the Garden Villa." He bowed. He was tuxedoed, wore white gloves, his jet black hair combed back. The tag said Philippines under his name. "Let me show you around your home for the next twelve days."

A real butler. Impressive. We followed him through the private cabana-lined pool and Jacuzzi area, into a living room with glass walls floor to ceiling. He pushed a button, and violet shades whirred in unison, closing out the world. We glided onto a deep blue carpet flocked with purple orchids. Plush cream couches and easy chairs filled the room. A huge flat screen TV and stereo system covered one wall. Pavarotti boomed out *"Nessun Dorma."* Fresh flowers adorned the cherry wood end tables.

I had resented Ashley and this hare-brained idea of a reconciliation cruise for our dying mom, but I was determined to take the high road. My last conversation with Mom had been so demeaning to me. She railed on and on how I was the cause of the divorce from my ex like his affairs had nothing to do with it. That was six weeks ago. Now here we were. I took a deep breath, smiled at my sister and my over-lipsticked mother and said, "This place is incredible. Thanks, Ashley."

Mr. Christopher, the butler, led us into a dining room and kitchen, and showed us how to use the espresso machine.

The bedrooms fanned off the living room. I was incredibly relieved to see we each had our own bedroom. The bathrooms had jetted tubs and showers in front of floor-to-ceiling windows that clung to the edge of the ship facing the ocean.

"Come, ladies." Christopher showed us to the main patio, where a lunch of fresh fruit, juices, and small sandwiches in the shape of shells and stars awaited us.

"Relax. I unpack your luggage." And with a soft smile, he disappeared.

"What do you think?" Ashley placed some grapes and a starfish-shaped sandwich on her plate and slid onto one of the deck chairs.

"Think?" I sighed, grabbed a drink with a flowered umbrella in it and plopped onto a chair next to Ashley.

"I contributed two thousand dollars for this trip, expecting a simple balcony room. I could never afford this." I waved my hands, then had an awful thought. "And is that butler going to touch my panties?"

"He puts panties away for a living. As to the money, plastic surgeons make mounds of it. Miles did well. You know that. The upgrade is on me."

I remembered well my sister's perfect marriage. Her life had been wonderful. Almost. Sadly, her wealthy and much older plastic-surgeon husband had indulged in one too many pounds of bacon and sausage over the years, wouldn't stop smoking, and had keeled over of a heart attack a year ago while having dinner on a cruise ship, leaving Ashley a very young forty-five-year-old rich widow…not to mention the best nipped and tucked face and body in Southern California.

So here we were, in our surprise suite, me, my older sister, ten years my senior, and my crazy mother. And, as Ashley so delightfully stated the day she'd handed us our cruise packets, "We're going to have a great time together or die trying."

I had my own reason for the cruise. My big surprise, my real father, Mario Carapelli, was waiting for me in Italy at our first port, Naples. I hoped that one of the holes in my heart would be filled.

Tony

Though Tony knew a relationship was the last thing he needed, the up-tick in his heart defied such logic. He noticed her at the check-in line. The canopied room for processing appeared chaotic with line after line of eager passengers. However, from past cruises, he knew order lurked beneath.

He moved forward, wishing he could cut in front of the two couples ahead of him. He kept her in sight. She stood next to two other women. The willowy and sophisticated blonde seemed to be in charge. The rock on her left hand was blinding. The older woman appeared frail, as though a gust of ocean wind could blow her overboard. Perhaps the mother of the blonde? They had the same aquiline nose, enormous cobalt blue eyes and shoulder-length hair, the older one's hair thinning. The frail woman's eyes were watery and the lines on her face suggested a hard life. Her unfashionable clothes were in stark contrast to the Vogue-attired perfection of the younger woman. His work demanded he notice details, and at times like this it annoyed him.

The woman who caught his eye was the short, curvaceous woman with the dark hair and Elizabeth Taylor eyes. He'd been observing her for a good ten minutes. Her gray gaze was solemn. She lifted her chin slightly in response to something the blonde said. One of his skills was the ability to read facial expressions. It was obvious she was experiencing a crisis of some kind. Her smile never quite reached her eyes. And she kept fingering something in the pocket of her slacks.

The woman turned, caught his careful study of her, and lowered her head.

He looked away, then back. Her defiance was clear from the way she pursed her lips. She rolled her shoulders back and forth, and twisted her hair.

The three women collected their room keys and made their way to the gangplank. He assumed they'd be in the same area of the ship since they were all in the "Suite" line. He enjoyed the swing of the younger women's hips as they walked away.

"Next, please." A dark-haired woman with a soft voice called him to the number four window. Her name tag indicated she was Maria, from Rome.

"*Ciao, Maria. Come va?*" He handed her an envelope containing his passport, travel documents, and cabin reservation along with copies of his luggage tags.

Her chestnut eyes glowed when he spoke to her in Italian. The paperwork rustled while she checked each document. He checked his surroundings while she processed the papers. She clicked them together with a stapler.

"*Signore Canali.* Welcome aboard." The clerk returned his passport along with a room key.

"Everything is in order, sir. Have a wonderful cruise."

"*Grazie,*" he responded, flashing a smile.

So far, so good. This assignment required he blend in. But he'd been told there was no one available to pair with him. As a joke, he'd proposed the idea of hiring an "under-cover wife." All he'd received in return was a cold stare and an abrupt "no." A smile tugged at the corner of his lips as he remembered his boss's face.

Dodging the aggressive ship photographers in front of the "Welcome Aboard" sign, he headed straight to his room and inserted the key card for the Emerald Suite, Room 11704. He'd insisted on an even-numbered room. Made him more comfortable. Ever since he was a kid, odd numbers bothered him. To a person who'd always paid attention to details, even numbers seemed better orga-nized, something completed. He was pleased with his high deck. Deck 11 suited him fine.

The room mirrored the photo and floor plan he'd received two weeks ago from the headquarters of NeroMare, Ltd. He found the second room, the one for a family shar-ing the suite, and checked the closet for his equipment. Everything he needed was properly placed…the computer, private cell phone, gun, and a file containing pertinent documents for this assignment.

Dropping his overnight on the floor, he took off his jacket and dressed in the casual linen pants and shirt wait-ing in the closet. As instructed, Tony made his way to the pool deck for the sail-away party.

When he was offered the drink of the day, a Blue Lagoon, he bought it and hid behind the frothy blue concoction as he walked the deck, busy eyes behind his sleek Prada sunglasses. He took a quick sip, noting it was long on blue Curacao and short on vodka.

He flicked his gaze across the deck and spotted the three women. He ambled toward them and leaned on the railing far enough to observe, close enough to hear.

The one he found attractive had a melodious laugh that pleased him. Then a tall white-uniformed officer from the ship blocked his view.

It's a twelve day cruise. I'll see her again.

"See anything yet, other than a female to tame your loins?"

Tony felt himself jump inside, but his body never moved. "Don't be crass," he said, relieved to make contact with his handler.

The man warned him. "Watch yourself. Women might be involved in this, not to mention the danger you might put them in." The voice was monotone, void of emotion and tamed of any accent. The man was of medium height, thin legs, but his upper body was a tight network of muscles hidden beneath loose-fitting clothes, his face unmemorable, except for the coldness of his pale blue eyes.

"Everything seems to be in order in my room," Tony said.

"It's been swept clean. Just make sure no one goes near the extra room. Your butler has been working on board for two weeks. Cover story is he transferred from another ship."

"How do I contact you?" Tony glanced at him.

"You don't. Each day with breakfast, the butler, who works for me, will either hand you contact places on ship or shore, or text you where we'll meet. We've been placed at the same table for dinner but won't sit next to each other. It'll appear more natural that we say hello once in awhile if we're table mates."

This assignment was critical. A month ago, there had been a rise of the noro virus report on several cruise ships. His handler had sent him a memo about this particular ship. Over 500 passengers had been sickened with the virus and several people had died on the last cruise. It had raised suspicion that there could be something else going on.

Tony had studied the information along with the deck plans and crew serving in the kitchen and service areas, memorizing names and photos given to him. His agency had been contacted by the U. S. Government, who suspected stolen syringes from the CDC had gotten into the hands of someone who meant to do great harm on a ship whose passengers consisted mainly of United States citizens...even the possibility of a trial run at mass murder. This particular cruise line had had recent cases of over 1500 people hit with the virus on the last three ten-day cruises. Now people were dying, eight on the cruise before this one. And there was chatter these numbers would grow. The crew members were the main suspects. Tox reports had revealed a mysterious virus. Not his job to identify the virus. His job was to identify, if possible, a person or persons who may be on board with the syringes. This ship held 2200 passengers and 1,564 crew members.

Like looking for the needle in a haystack. He shrugged his shoulders and stared at the dock as the ship moved from Civitavecchia, the main port for Rome. As the band played *Arrivederci, Roma*, he turned to ask another question, but his handler had disappeared. Instead, Tony looked straight into the face of the dark-haired woman. She was staring at him. He turned his head, pretending to sip the now flat blue drink in his hand. He hid his unease when she engaged him in brief conversation. Wanting to see her eyes up close, he reached to remove her sunglasses. She stepped back, and he felt stupid. He was rewarded with the uncovering of silvery eyes. He excused himself and strolled across the deck to the elevator.

He had work to do. But he couldn't help himself. He took off his dark glasses and entered the lift. The woman stood at the rail, but turned to watch him. He nodded and noted the blush on her cheeks.

Just before the elevator door shut, he caught a glimpse of a tall expressionless cocktail waitress passing a note to one of the passengers dressed in a Hawaiian shirt, his hair covered by a Panama hat.

Tony exited the elevator and strolled toward the passenger. Neither the waitress nor the man spoke a word. He memorized their faces. The boss was right. He couldn't trust anyone, male or female. In ten seconds, doing what years of training had taught him, he'd memorized the faces of two potential suspects and his gray-eyed lady.

He again entered the elevator and pressed the button for Deck 11. For just a moment, loneliness tugged at him.

Olivia

I enjoyed a languid shower and readied myself for dinner. Having an hour before meeting Mom and Ashley, I fetched my briefcase from the dresser by the vanity and curled up on the couch. I unzipped the side pocket and pulled out the manila envelope holding the correspondence from Mario Carapelli, my father. It seemed unreal. The many grainy photos of him and his family from the time he was a child confirmed he was my birth father. I recognized my own features in his and the other family in the photograph and marveled at how I fit in with these strangers. They made a startling contrast to the light-haired and fair-skinned family who'd raised me.

Closing my eyes, I remembered the day Ashley and I had the 'big fight.' I was twelve, flat-chested, bony-kneed, and Ashley was golden-haired, sleek, smart and popular, twenty-two and free. Home for her last summer after college, every weekend boys in gleaming cars came to take her somewhere--to movies, dinner, shining beaches. Maybe to Xanadu, for all I knew.

Three or four times that summer, sleeping with my window open, I had heard the cars return, and murmuring voices, one of them Ash's, at the front door. Then the door would open and close quietly, and I would hear Ash's bare feet on the stairs.

Once I heard Dad's voice, and then Ash saying crossly, "Oh, Daddy," and he said, "two o'clock in the morning…" and she had said something. And then I heard her steps go down the hall toward her room, and Dad's to his and Mom's.

My father died six months later of a heart attack. His death exposed my mother's instability. Strong and steady, my dad had covered for mom by making excuses for why she cried or was tired. He protected her from herself and us. As I grew older, I learned about his true character.

I don't even remember what the fight was about. Somehow I'd made Ash furious. "You're adopted!" she'd screamed, her usually flawless complexion marred and blotchy.

"I am not," I protested, and crumbled in tears. It was a cruel awakening, making clear why I, the dark-haired, olive-skinned, gray-eyed sister always felt like I was on the outside looking in where my family was concerned. I always knew I looked different. But, adopted?

Mom slapped Ashley's face. "Go to your room. We'll talk later."

Mom turned to me and said, "Don't get hysterical. I'm your real mother and you are not adopted. I'll explain it later." She stalked out of the room to confront Ashley.

I never knew what happened between Ashley and Mom. I'd heard raised voices, followed by shrill yelling from my Mother.

Ashley came to me later in the day. "I'm sorry."

I looked at her. "Don't want to talk about it," I mumbled.

Somehow I managed to stuff my feelings, pretending everything was okay between us. From that day forward, I kept any sense of "feeling" deep inside myself, covered with a pretend cheerfulness I seldom felt.

Time passes and things change. My life became tolerable when Ashley went to live on campus for her last two years of college. We learned to accept each other, having in common the queen mother of dysfunction and drama.

During one of Ashley's winter breaks from college, mom shocked us during an afternoon conversation.

"Mom?" asked Ashley. "I thought you had stopped drinking."

Mom took another gulp of her wine then paused and looked thoughtfully at Ashley. "I try not to drink, but I need to tell both of you girls a secret. Don't ask questions. Because I have no answers." She sighed, placed her wine glass on the coffee table in the family room and rested her head on the back of the chair.

"When you were about ten or eleven, Ashley, I had an affair."

"What?" Ashley's face had turned white.

"I said not to ask questions," said mom. "Just listen. This man swept me off my feet," she'd said.

"But Dad?"

"I was lucky he didn't throw me out. But he did the right thing by you. He kept his mouth shut with the promise no one would ever know."

I remembered feeling numb, then afraid as my stomach tied itself in knots. "Who was he?"

"He'd worked for the Italian Consulate in Los Angles." She looked at me, tears gathering, and said, "You, Olivia, were his child. I never told him. He went back to Italy. End of story."

"But I deserve to know. Wait, how can you be sure?"

"Look at yourself, Olivia. Do you look like the rest of the family? That's all you need to know. And I can't tell you any more information. I'm sorry." She picked up her wine glass and finished it, walked out of the room and into her bedroom. The subject never came up again.

I had pursued my paternity from that day forward. I snooped into my mother's personal files and drawers and old photos, finding clue after clue. It took years and a lot of help from genealogy experts, and several crying confessions while mother was in one of her late-night maudlin drunks, to find Mario. Oddly, my ex, Jon, had been most helpful, using his computer skills to research the clues. I guess he felt helping me would relieve him of his guilt for ruining our marriage by walking out on me because he didn't love me anymore. Later, of course, I found out there were other women. Nevertheless, I was grateful for his help, anyone's help.

Not knowing my real dad had made the first couple years of our marriage difficult. I feared Jon would leave me some day as my father and birth father had. Made no sense, really. After the divorce, I'd realized I'd been nothing but eye candy for him and his business. I thought I'd put it to rest. My shrink had shown me how Jon had married me, and then commenced to mold me into what he thought I should be. He wanted to "fix" me. In therapy, I learned and accepted I was fine. Just made bad choices in men. During our last year married, as I grew in confidence, Jon seemed to rebel against my new-found spunk. He dumped me, flinging me right back to having trust issues again. He had affairs. I tolerated it for awhile. Then he hit me with the famous 'it's not you but me' line.

I removed the photo of my birth father from the pocket of my slacks, tears welling over the wasted years. But, as usual, I compartmentalized my emotions, tucking them away to deal with later, if at all.

The three of us strolled to the penthouse elevator, and I pushed the "Deck Six" button. We navigated our way to the Summer Palace at the back of the ship.

The manager of this restaurant, a tall, thin woman in a tailored navy blue suit, wearing horn-rimmed spectacles that looked amazing on her, asked for our room key. Her name was Marina with a last name of mostly consonants and the country of Slovenia on her name tag. She reached out to shake Ashley's hand. "Ah, yes. Mrs. Morgan-Brown.

Welcome back to Princess Cruises and to our dining room. We have a special table for you by the window." She waved her hand, and a handsome Slavic waiter with another unpronounceable name, led us to a table at the back of the dining room, where two couples were already seated. Ah, drat. I was in no mood for small talk with strangers tonight.

We sat, smiling politely. Ashley took the first step in the babbling intros.

"Ashley Morgan-Brown," she said, reaching to shake hands. "This is my sister, Olivia and my mother, Veronica."

I dreaded the responses, imagining...Mr. and Mrs. We're Happily Married and celebrating thirty years of wedded bliss, blah, blah, blah.

We made introductions around the table.

There was a chorus of 'nice to meet you's.'

Our waiter glided to our table, handed us menus, then introduced himself. He stood tall and blond, his smile dazzling. His clear blue eyes sparkled. His name tag indicated he was from Latvia. Latvia? Latvia might have been on Mars for all I knew.

Another waiter asked for drink orders. Each of the couples ordered a bottle of wine. Ashley ordered a fancy French burgundy, Chassaugne Montrachet.

While others perused the menu, I settled on a simple meal of salad, broiled chicken and vegetables, and took the opportunity to take in the room. The floor-to-ceiling glass windows offered stunning sea views of the setting sun and a golden glow behind the clouds. The draperies framing the windows were a soft yellow with deep red trim and rich gold tassels. The heavy window treatment muffled the chatter of the room into a soft din. White table linens were paired with deep burgundy napkins which accented the polished silver and twinkling crystal glasses. Delicious aromas suggested soon-to-be-served pasta and a hint of French onion soup. The array of silverware by my plate glistened as though newly polished. I didn't know which one to use first—outside in, maybe–and wondered whatever happened to a simple spoon, knife, and fork.

Someone called my name.

"Sorry, I was day-dreaming again. What did you say?" I politely waited until my table mate re-asked his question.

"I said I can't believe you're sisters...you look so different."

"We have different fathers."

Ashley's pointed-toe Jimmy Chu shoes nicked my leg.

I muffled an 'ouch.' "Just kidding. You know how gene pools are? Sometimes everyone in the family looks like they're cloned from a single gene and other families get a little bit of mom, dad, grandparents, someone of unknown origins in the woodpile..."

Thankfully, the wine steward arrived with our drinks.

I looked up to see the man I'd seen at the sail-away. Something fluttered around the hard knot in my stomach. *Was he sitting with us?* I followed him with my eyes as he took a seat at the end of the table.

"Sorry I'm late." He introduced himself with his faint but distinct accent, which I'd identified as Brooklyn.

"*Ciao.* My name is Antonio Canali. Most people call me Tony. I hail from New York. Brooklyn, to be specific."

He smiled. Dear God. That smile. Those lips.

"Hi, Tony." I felt a crack in the brittle but firm emotional shell I'd built around my heart. *Nice name. I've wanted you from the moment I saw you leaning on the railing.*

The small talk at the table perked along during dinner. The waiter and his assistant served us, appearing like genies, quietly deferential. I could get used to this.

Ashley, though, troubled me. After living apart for so many years, I sensed a flaw in her perfect façade. Her pure elegance fell silent with each sip of wine. Not that she ever slurred her words or became loud and obnoxious. It seemed to be more insidious...sort of like a perfect wind-up toy that spun around with perfection and toddled as it ran out of energy. Her posture slumped ever so slightly. My older sister had a fragility I'd not seen before. Yet she blended into the conversation with the two couples as though Miles were right there beside her, joining in.

Drinking had not been an indulgence of mine. My husband, I had labeled him 'the Plaintiff 'during the divorce proceedings, reveled in the attention when the nipped and tucked beauties flirted with him...enjoying it too much for my taste. He only indulged in these flirtations after several drinks. I'd become used to avoiding alcohol to keep an eye on him. Having a wildly successful real estate business in

Newport Beach required much entertaining, being seen, etc. Why had I never noticed his flirting at these events?

A yelp from the other end of the table interrupted my thoughts. Jim, the one with Jill, let out an "Oh my gosh." Seeing my curious expression, he turned to us. "I just found out Sam and Sandy are part of the dance club on board."

A gasp caught in my throat. "A dance club? You mean like real Arthur Murray stuff?" The Plaintiff loomed in my mind, and the knot in my stomach hardened again. The plaintiff—my ex–Jonathan Hillman II could dance anyone under the table. Dancing for me was a sport to be endured. I loved the music, the rhythm, the movement. But the right foot always disappeared, and another left foot grew whenever I attempted this elegant coupling of a man and a woman. Dance and Club were like Torture and Death.

Ashley took a sip of wine. "Isn't that wonderful? Miles and I used to dance all the time."

"Excuse me." A Putin-looking man appeared near the empty seat across from Tony. His muscles bulged under his tan sport jacket, making it seem a size too small. His eyes were an icy blue.

"I guess this is my table. Sorry I'm late, but I fell asleep. Jet lag!" He nodded in our direction. "My name is Joe." He turned to the waiter, who appeared out of nowhere, and said, "I'll have a coffee."

There was something about his eyes. They were calculating, like those of a hunter. His voice, raspy and slightly threatening, made me uneasy. I made a mental note to avoid sitting near him at future dinners.

I managed to fumble through dinner, taking part in the conversation and guiltily interjecting a few words here and there, mostly in response to questions. An overwhelming need to escape and get away from the "getting to know you" chatter overcame me.

"Great meeting all of you." I placed my napkin on the table. Immediately, the waiter appeared, helping me with my chair.

"Thank you."

He bowed. "You're quite welcome, madam."

"Where are you going, Olivia?" My sister sounded disappointed at my sudden departure.

"To my room to freshen up before the show tonight." I flashed my sister a smile.

My mom stood up, yawning. "Can I go with you, dear? I'm ready for bed."

"No problem."

I waved, and slowed down for my mom. She was true to her word, walking into her room and closing the door. I made a quick retreat to my room. Alone with my thoughts, I curled up on my now-favorite chair and gazed at the white foam of the sea. Fighting tears, I cursed Jon for the divorce and myself for being so blind about his indiscretions. I cursed my sister for her hare-brained idea of a cruise to heal our family. I picked up the photo of my real father, and silently blasted my mom for keeping him from me.

Thirty minutes later, my pity party over, I strolled to the mirror, applied lipstick and another quick spray of *Profuma Roma,* and headed to the elevator.

Might as well go watch the dancers while waiting for the show.

The theater was on the fourth deck at the bow of the ship. I walked into its lushness admiring the softly lit crystal chandeliers, and sank into a plush red velvet seat near the back. The theater was massive. The ship band was playing a classic tune from the big band era, "When They Begin the Beguine" as the dance-club couples flooded the floor, gliding and turning. And after watching them briefly, I concluded some of them should have saved the money they'd spent on lessons.

But the best couples moved together with a romantic grace, part of a world from which I was now excluded.

I felt a strong warm hand on my shoulder. Tony sat on the arm of the seat in back of me and asked, "Why so glum?"

"Glum? It's that obvious, huh?" I smiled wanly. "Still difficult for me to function in a couples' world. Give me a moment of utter bitterness, and I'll be okay."

Tony laughed. "Come on. The band is playing a slow tune. 'Harbor Lights,' isn't it?"

"You're kidding me, right? You didn't see my face turn white when our tablemates revealed being part of a dance club?" I looked down and pointed. "See my two left feet?"

He took my hand and gently pulled me from my seat. "You've never danced with me." His voice resonated, deep and seductive.

"Whatever."

His guiding hand on my lower back felt like a searing iron. He gently moved me into his arms and led me a few steps. Mortified at my clumsiness, I rested my head on his shoulder and gave myself to the rhythm of the music.

His arms felt muscular. He smelled of soap and a hint of cologne like rainy woods. I breathed in the pure maleness of him. When the music stopped, my disappointment surprised me. My body was sizzling. It had been a long time since a man held me in his arms.

"See, Olivia, you can dance." He winked, took my hand, and walked me to the back of the theater just as the band broke into "Boogie Woogie Bugle Boy."

"I'm sorry, Tony. I can't stop daydreaming. I think jet-lag has taken its toll on me." I frowned and asked, "By the way, did you get a weird feeling about the guy who joined us at dinner tonight? He gave me the creeps."

"Well, I'm sure he's a stand-up guy. After all, we only saw him for fifteen minutes."

A commotion at the theater entrance distracted us. A group of women I guessed to be seventy to eightyish in red and purple polyester pants and those gaudy feather-infested red hats gathered into a group, laughing. Silk scarves of crimson and varying shades of purple waved from necks and arms, and peeked out bravely from Rubenesque cleavage.

I covered my mouth to hold in the laughter. "Okay, Tony. Those are the Red Hat Ladies. And I'm going on record to say I will go to my grave hatless."

"They're just gals who want to have fun." He tucked his finger under my chin. "You need more of that."

I glanced at the group of blindingly bright ladies. I had to admit, for a brief moment, I envied their obvious fun.

Behind the blur of purple and red ladies, I saw a sea of neon green. T-shirts swarmed into the theater ranging in age from babies to elders cruising in walkers. Emblazoned in fuchsia on their shirts were the words "Johnson Family Reunion, May, 2014."

I wondered if it could get any worse. First a dance club, then the ravishing-red-hat ladies, and now a hellish happy family. "Tony, I really need to go to my room. I'm sleepy and don't have a happy spirit right now."

"I'll walk you to the elevator."

And then it got worse.

"Olivia! Olivia, I have someone I want you to meet." It was Ashley's high-pitched voice. I tried to ignore her.

"Olivia, didn't you hear me?" Her voice screeched like bad brakes.

"What?" I snapped.

"I want to introduce you to Captain Anders Kildal."

I beamed a smile as the Captain approached. "A pleasure to meet you, Captain." I reached out to shake his hand. "And this is Tony."

"Pleased to meet both of you." Captain Kildal's cobalt blue eyes were as compelling as his gold braided white uniform. "The first formal night, you will be receiving an invitation to my table. I hope you will join me."

He spoke English well, but all his w's sounded like v's. As in "You vill be…"

"May I bring Tony?"

Ashley tossed me a perturbed glance. "It's just for the Garden Villa Suites." She turned to the Captain. "Olivia is unsure of protocol." She smiled while patting my arm like I was a misbehaving puppy.

My teeth clenched. Tony rested his hand on my other arm and squeezed it gently. I said nothing.

"Captain," Tony said, bowing. "I already received my invitation. I'm Tony Canali."

The captain paused, a shadow of concern and recognition on his face. "Ah yes, Mr. Canali. In the Emerald Suite. I've been looking forward to meeting you."

The Captain knew of him. Who the heck was Tony?

"I'm going to excuse myself." I turned to Ashley. "The cruise guide says the show will be televised tomorrow in our rooms. I can't keep my eyes open."

"I'm going to pass on the show tonight, too," said Tony. "I have some computer work to do."

Ashley turned without a word and hooked her arm in the Captain's, and let Anders whatever escort her to a seat.

Tony laughed. "If I tipped at you with my little finger, you'd fall over. I'm jetlagged, too."

His cell phone rang. His answers to the caller were clipped and secretive. A string of "uh huh's," a "see you there," and he placed the phone into his shirt pocket.

We walked to the private elevator in the middle of the ship. He slipped his key in the slot, pushed the floor button with a tanned finger, and we rose toward Deck 11. The door slid open. Tony touched my shoulder. "I'll see you at dinner tomorrow if not before." With a wink, he was gone.

I brushed my teeth, slipped into my gown and robe, and sat on my balcony breathing in the sea air. Something nagged at me. I sat upright. The voice. Tony had held the phone away from his ear, and I clearly heard the voice on the other end. It was a familiar voice, deep, with an East Coast accent. Joe, the James-Bond-movie-bad-guy at our table tonight. His firm yet icy voice was unmistakable. Nah. Impossible. I shook off the thought, went back into the bedroom and fetched my phone. There was a text waiting for me.

"*Isola di Capri* tomorrow. I'll be on the patio in front of Quisinino's Hotel, wearing a yellow sweater. Mario."

Christopher

He entered his small windowless room, flipped the light switch and flopped onto his bed, exhausted from his twelve-hour day.

"I'll rest a minute," he whispered.

But once he closed his eyes, he fell into a deep sleep. The shrill bell tone of his secret phone jarred him awake.

He rolled off his bed and stumbled to his safe in the tiny corner closet. Christopher shook his head and rolled his shoulders while twisting the dial, trying to clear his brain. He grabbed the phone.

"Yes?" He asked.

"You alone? Safe to talk?"

Chris looked at his watch. "It's two a.m. I was sleeping."

"Sorry," said Tony. "This is important. Our contact spotted Alejandro and Danelo passing information to each other in the staff rec room. Since tomorrow's port is Naples, we suspect something is going down."

"I hope so. I'm damn tired of making beds and cleaning toilet bowls."

"And I appreciate how clean you keep my cabin." Tony chuckled. "It's nice to be served for a change. I'll be sure to leave you an extra twenty for your service."

"Get on with the crap. Tomorrow is my whopping half day of freedom in port. Who do I follow?"

"You need to stay in character. What's with the mouth?"

"Hey, I was born in Brooklyn, grew up on the streets...I'm an American playing a role."

"Then stay in it. Even when you talk to me. Now here's the scoop. I think Carmella is involved…waitress in the Atrium bar, port side. She's also been cozying up to a bizarre loud-mouth passenger who always wears a hat."

"Oh yeah. He hangs out in the cigar lounge. Pudgy, always wearing flowered Hawaiian shirts? Gives a whole new meaning to "Ugly American.""

Tony laughed. "That's him." He paused. "Chris, you've pulled out of your persona a couple of times in the hallway. Keep the accent; use your Tagalog language skills more. Throw in a casual *musta* and *gudnayt* to a crew member once in awhile. And stay aloof. At all times!"

"Whatever." Chris leaned against the closet door. "Can I go back to sleep now?"

"Just be ready to disembark immediately. I cannot stress how important it is to be off the ship before the others. We have the two guys covered. Follow Carmella."

"Got it." Chris yawned.

"And, Chris?"

"Yes, sir."

"Focus. No flirting with the women, no drinking other than water and coffee, and don't forget your phone."

"You done, Tony?"

"Go back to sleep, Chris. I hope my substitute butler makes my bed as nicely as you do."

"Son of a…." But Tony had clicked off his phone.

Chris stripped down to his shorts, turned off the lights and crawled back into bed. He couldn't wait to get started on this assignment. He wanted nothing more than to succeed and get his long-awaited promotion. Visions of Carmella's face floated in his head; he'd memorized her features, her walk, and every trait that would help him follow her.

Day Two
Port Of Naples
Gateway To Pompei, Isle Of
Capri, And Amalfi Coast
Christopher

The rumbling and groaning ship along with the clanging and jarring of the lowering anchor startled a deep sleeping Christopher. The crew quarters on the third deck weren't exactly the quietest place on the ship.

Chris rolled out of bed, showered, shaved, and donned a white t-shirt and beige shorts. He checked his reflection in the miniscule mirror, smoothed his dark hair with some gel and tucked his cell phone into the front pocket of his shorts. Chris surveyed his room, declared it clear, and ran to the mess hall where he stuffed a roll and an apple in his other pocket and grabbed a water bottle.

"Feel like I'm living in a mail box," he muttered to no one. "Even my tiny apartment in Brooklyn beats this. Hate this assignment." He stuck his ear piece in place and headed for the gangplank area.

Customs was in the process of clearing the ship for disembarkation. He leaned against the wall near the check-out point, fourth in line. His dark eyes darted, looking for Carmella in the waiting line.

The Port of Naples pulsed with activity, boisterous vendors already offering their goods. The pungent smell of fresh fish blotted out any other scents. People screamed, yelled, and jostled each other to move, while *la dogana,* the Italian Immigration, stood at guard, carefully eyeing the activity next to the ship, and the *carabiniere* had their hands on their rifles.

Christopher loved the Italians, especially the people of Naples. He felt a kinship to them as a Filipino; the rhythm of life reminded him of the chaos in Manila when he visited his grandparents.

The Captain gave an all clear to disembark.

Chris pushed his card in the slot to prove his exit and ambled down the plank, looking for a spot to stand and watch for Carmella. He located the ticket shed for ferry boats going to various points along the Amalfi coast and leaned against the side, peering through dark sunglasses, observing the personnel. Everyone looked different out of uniform.

Carmella appeared, wearing a simple yellow sundress that would forbid her entrance into any Catholic church in Naples. Her long silky black hair hung straight down her back. On board, she wore her hair pulled back from her face, and her hair gathered into a bun. He watched as her eyes scanned the dock before she covered them with black sunglasses.

"She is one sexy lady." He spoke out loud without realizing it and a passing staff member stopped to look at him.

"Just talking to myself." Christopher smiled, and turned. Carmella had disappeared.

He searched the length of the dock, exited to the main square and caught a glimpse of the yellow sundress. He ran, zeroed in, breathing a sigh of relief.

Concentrate, you idiot.

Carmella spoke to no one. She strolled until she came to the incredible Galleria Umberto of Naples, an exquisite enclosed shopping center with marble floors and columns in early Roman design covered with a glass cupola.

At eight a.m. the store fronts were still shuttered, but the cafes were crammed with Italian businessmen and women enjoying their morning *cappuccinos* and *cornettos.* Carmella chose a table at *Caffetteria Vesuvio* and sat down. The cafe had a large seating area with great views of the mall. The aroma of the famous *Napolitano* coffee swirled around Christopher. He told himself this would be easy. No long walks through the winding streets of Naples, close to the ship, not a problem.

He sat a few tables behind her, ordered his coffee, a sweet roll and watched.

An hour later, the first tour groups appeared. Pods of thirty to forty people huddled around their guides. The galleria was permeated with smells of coffee and Italian breakfast rolls, now mingled in with perfumes and colognes, and bodies.

He heard him before he saw him. The obnoxious pudge with the hat. His hands flailing as he dominated his tour group with questions. Mr. Loud Mouth excused himself to use the toilette and managed to lose the group. He casually sat at a table next to Carmella. Soon they were engaged in conversation.

Chris dug the phone from his pocket and turned on his earpiece.

"Ciao, Chris. What's happening?"

"Tony, you were right. She's with the boisterous tourist with the flowered shirt. He managed to dump his tour group. They're at the *Caffetteria Vesuvio* sipping a cap, each sitting at their own table. He's doing the talking. He's also holding a flier about the Galleria. I see a strip of yellow paper inserted in the pamphlet. Bet my life she'll take a photo of it. Question is, what the heck do they have in common? What's the gig? They certainly don't look like 'let's-put-a-toxic-virus-in-the-food types'." He paused. "One more thing, Tony. I've heard the crew talk about him. He's a generous tipper. I don't think he's our guy but is here to gain confidence of the crew for some reason."

"Isn't your job to make judgment? Stay close. I'm at the *Brasiliano* across the way, reading *La Stampa*. The bus tours from Globus just pulled up outside. In fifteen minutes this place will be crawling with tour groups."

Christopher was distracted by the appearance of two cabin stewards, Danelo and Alejandro, sauntering through the Galleria and onto the main piazza. They were being followed by two other men, guys with thick necks and round Slavic faces, business suits, definitely tailing the cabin stewards.

"Tony, can you see the muscle following the stews?"

"Got 'em. You concentrate on Carmella and photo that note. Those guys are Russian. I hope we haven't been dropped into a situation with the *Camorra*. Later."

Chris sauntered over to Carmella's table, and casually turned on his phone camera snapped a photo just as the big flowered-shirt guy stood up. He waved and left. Carmella looked around, placed the note in the pamphlet, and grabbed her purse.

Chris smiled at Carmella. "Wow, you look gorgeous with your hair down." He picked up the pamphlet.

"What's this?" he asked.

"I think it describes this Galleria Umberto." Carmella's voice wobbled. "I was going to take it."

"No. Look. It has a coffee stain on it. I'll grab a new one for you from the stand." He walked to the tourist info case and took a new one.

"Here you are," he said. "Looks like it'll be a beautiful day. I have a few hours off. Think I'll head over to Capri. What are your plans? You working the Atrium bar tonight?"

"Yes." She smiled weakly.

"See you on board." He walked to the exit.

"You get it?" Tony's voice rasped through his hidden ear piece.

"Yup. I'm sending it right now. Looks like Gambrinus Café is where the action is. At least they're choosing a classy place. Carmella seems jittery. She just lit up her fourth cigarette."

"Wander around. I'll check out the info."

"See you around, boss. What I want to know is what the hell the Filipinos and the toxin have in common." Chris strolled to a newsstand and bought a paper. Raking his hand through his hair, and taking a deep breath, he started to walk aimlessly, waiting for Tony's next instructions.

Chris held his phone and kept walking, looking neither left nor right. He didn't see the big Hawaiian shirt guy coming at him from the sidewalk. Christopher felt a thump as the man hit his arm. He slipped.

"I'm so sorry, sir," the man said in a quiet but firm voice. "I wasn't watching where I was going. Clumsy of me. Are you okay? Your walk is a bit wobbly."

"I'm fine," said Christopher, his vision blurring. He knew the guy had lifted the pamphlet, not knowing he'd already taken a photo and sent it with a text.

"Let's head down this alley. I see a café where you can sit until you feel better."

Christopher leaned against the brick building, faking a faint and slumped to the ground.

The man took out his cell phone, hit send.

"Yeah?"

"There's a man who fainted in the first alley off the main street in front of Gambrinus. Find him. You know what to do. I don't think they have the location. I lifted the paper he took from Carmello."

He wandered off, not looking back. He also failed to notice Christopher standing up and walking down the alley. Chris took his cell phone and notified Tony about the threat. "Said he was sending some thugs to take care of me."

"Get out of there, fast. I'll watch to see if anyone comes."

Ten minutes later, three men approached the alley. Christopher was gone. One of the men made a call on his cell. They left.

Tony was puzzled. The three men were obviously Italian mafia. He knew them well. Their intention was to "take out" Chris. What did the passenger on the boat have to do with them?

Christopher circled the piazza and walked back toward the ship. He approached the booth where he'd been waiting earlier that morning and purchased a ticket to the Isle of Capri.

"Might as well see something pretty today," he murmured to himself. He boarded the hydrofoil, found a seat in the furthest corner in the back, and settled in for the forty-minute ride. He checked the text he'd sent Tony. The note simply announced a time and place.

"Gambrinus Café, 6 p.m. Chinese."

Olivia

From the top of the ship I could see all of Naples. I'm not a morning person, but to avoid dealing with my family, I'd had room service deliver my coffee and brioche at six a.m. It was that or wear a shirt that says, "Don't talk to me before I've had my coffee." Most of the time, another line should be added. "...actually, don't talk to me then either."

Convincing Mom and Ash to see Pompeii today without me had been difficult.

"Olivia," Mom whined. "We're supposed to be together."

But I'd convinced them I could not tolerate a tour just yet and preferred to linger close to the ship, promising them some shopping on the Isle of Capri tomorrow. Naples was an overnight port. Convenient for my little white lie.

Raising my binoculars, I focused on the ticket booths on the left of the ship's disembarkation ramp. As Mario had said, there were clearly marked signs for boats to Capri.

I finished my coffee and hurried to get ready for the day. I walked to the mirror, spritzed some classic *Dolce e Gabbana* on my neck, checked my makeup in the gold leafed mirror over my dresser, and took a deep breath. I wore white Capris with a soft yellow blouse. Mario said he'd be wearing yellow, too. Yellow? For a manly man?

"Here I come, Mario...Dad." My stomach felt as though a thousand frantic hummingbirds had been released. I threw back my shoulders and walked to the elevator, praying the ding of the bell would not awaken my mother.

I hovered in the atrium by the gangway waiting for the all clear announcement from customs. When the announcement was made, I keyed in my card at the exit, walked down the ramp...always avoiding the ever-present ship photographers..., and strolled to the ticket booth. I purchased my round trip tickets to *Isola di Capri*, too nervous to think, forgetting to breathe.

I climbed the narrow winding staircase to the top of the boat and found a seat near the rail. To my relief, the eight a.m. boat was quiet. No ship people or tour groups this early. The vessel plowed through the waves, splashing salt spray on my hair and face.

I closed my eyes and rested my head against the back of the seat. My search for my birth father had taken so many strange turns. It started with the locket my mom began to wear after my "father's" death. One day when she was sleeping off a drinking binge, I'd crept into her room, lifted the locket from her nightstand and opened it. I remembered a feeling of shock when I saw the photo inside. The man was young and handsome. But it was his curly hair and light eyes peeping from his bronzed face that had stunned me. It was my face echoing back at me. My first clue. With trembling hands, I'd returned the locket to the stand and tiptoed from the room, shaking, knowing now the face of my birth father. Now to discover his name.

Another afternoon I'd snuck into her office and had carefully gone through her files. In the back of the bottom file drawer, behind thick folders, I'd found a stack of notes tied with a red ribbon. I slid one note from the pile. The words made me blush. They were intimate, sensual, and were signed in Italian.

Ti voglio bene. Mario

Mario. I'd rolled the name over my tongue. It wasn't until years later when I studied Italian I learned how precious that phrase was in its meaning. Its literal meaning was…I want you good. Made no sense. Then I discovered it was a strong idiomatic version of…I love you.

The boat horn announced the imminent arrival to Capri and shook me out of my reverie.

The island came into view. It was as though Capri were a grand rock jammed into the Tyrrhenian Sea. The turquoise water shimmered, edges of deep purple jutting into the blue water. Jewel tones seemed to drape like silk scarves from the houses perched precariously on the cliffs.

The boat jammed itself against a pier bustling with people boarding ferries back to Naples and other ports nearby. Tourists scrambled for taxis.

"Focus, Olivia. Focus on his directions."

I ambled down the long pier until I saw the signs for the *funicolare*, the railway incline into Ana Capri. As Mario promised, the line was short at this hour. I'd never been on an incline and felt queasy looking straight up the side of this island.

An attractive Italian woman hustled me and others onto one of the cars. The vistas as we ascended were spectacular, the perfume of the flowers growing beside the rails delicious, the deepening sea colors amazing. And Mario waiting for me.

I turned left onto the main street and followed it to the end, oblivious of the shops or the people. My eyes were on the prize. My father. The man whose DNA had made me a stark contrast to the family I'd lived with all these years.

The letters were blurred from the folding and unfolding of the email. "We'll meet on the Isle of Capri at Quisisanos. Everyone knows it. Just ask. I think you will know me. I'll be wearing yellow. You'll see my face and recognize the eyes and chin. I've yearned for this time. To touch you, see you, will be my life's greatest treasure. *Con molto affetto*, Mario."

Glancing at my watch, I noted I was fifteen minutes early. Quisisano Hotel loomed white and elegant, the five stars of brass gleaming in the sunlight. In the furthest corner of the patio, under the last flag to the left, sat a man with thick silver and black hair, eyes hidden by stylish Gucci sunglasses. Tied around his shoulders over a classic blue and white pin striped shirt was a bright yellow sweater. Very Newport Beach. And, as I would soon discover, very Italian. I sucked in a breath, paused, and walked toward him. He removed his glasses.

A glimmer of sunlight blinked through the trees and bounced across the marble patio floor. I felt an electric shock pierce through me. I was looking at my own face. Gray eyes rimmed with green, the wavy dark hair, straight nose.

His eyes were bright with tears matching mine. He walked to me with long strides.

"Olivia." His voice was breathy in my ear. He held me tightly to him. "Olivia. Olivia."

My body felt warm and cozy as though I'd been out in a cold storm, lost, but was now at home in a room of sunshine and safety.

After an embrace that seemed to last a lifetime, he pulled me away and moved his hands to hold my face and gazed into my eyes. Neither of us could speak.

"Come sit with me, Olivia. We have so much to talk about."

We settled into the plush white and blue chairs, unable to stop staring at each other.

The familiarity removed the edge from the awkwardness.

Mario pushed aside the *La Stampa* and took my hand. "You're beautiful. More beautiful than your pictures." His smile revealed even white teeth.

"I'm not photogenic like you, though," I said.

"*Mio Dio*, I've missed so many years. If I'd known you existed...if only I'd known." His eyes filled once again.

"Well, now I know where I get my raw emotions." Tears welled in my eyes, too.

We both laughed.

"It'll take time, Mario. Time to know each other. Just talk to me." The awkward feeling returned. My stomach in knots, I told myself over and over he never knew I existed. And anger was rearing its ugly head once again, at a mother who'd lied to me.

"Your mother was young, Olivia. I see the cloud of anger in your eyes. I knew she was married. For me, it was a romantic adventure in Los Angeles, a beautiful blonde with eyes the color of the sky. It was a magical three months. She was unhappy, Olivia."

"My mother has always been unhappy. She's an alcoholic. She uses people and drinks…and she's dying. And right now, I feel like a lost little girl. And I hate that feeling. Don't want to talk about my mother." My hands gripped the cup of espresso the waiter had just delivered. I wanted to throw the cup at anyone. *Should I have let this rest? Maybe this had all been a huge mistake.*

Mario tilted my defiant chin with his finger tips. "I want to see your mother."

"Are you crazy?" I half stood, realized I'd yelled, and sat back down.

"It's for you, *caramia*. You need closure, forgiveness, and so does your mother." His face hardened, erasing the gentleness of his voice. "If you want a relationship with me, we all have to fix this lie. Family is everything, Olivia. Don't fight me on this."

He mumbled something under his breath in the Napolitano dialect. I knew the words. They weren't nice. And I mumbled right back at him.

"You have my introverted temper and sarcasm."

"Really? A temper? Introverted? Interesting." I leaned toward him. "So, Daddy, tell me all about you and Mummy. Was she a drunk back then, too?"

"Olivia, don't be disrespectful." He paused, studying his hands. He gulped the remaining espresso and turned to me. "I would tell you it was all a big mistake. But then, you wouldn't be here, would you?"

What the heck was the matter with me? I was taking out my anger towards Mom and slamming it onto my newly found father.

"I'm sorry for my remarks." I touched his cheek. "Please, tell me. I'll listen with an open mind." I folded my hands on my lap and stared at them. "I had no right to talk to you with such disrespect. But I feel like a little girl right now. Do you understand?"

"*Si*, Olivia. Now listen. It began when I was assigned to the Italian Embassy in LA, ready for a good time in

America. I was so young, my first time away from home. No one was watching me when I left work. And Los Angeles was *pieno*, full of people and excitement compared to my small town in Italy. I had been promised to my childhood sweetheart, Angela." He paused to take a breath.

With my chin resting on my left hand and my right hand holding my now tepid espresso, I listened...for a long time.

Christopher

Chris stopped dead when he saw Olivia sitting spellbound listening to this stunning Italian man. He hit Tony's number on his cell.

"Hey, I'm walking past the good old Quisi's and who do I see? Your lady, Olivia, chatting up a hunky older Italian. Old enough to be her pops."

"And you called me, why?"

"Wondered how it's going. Not too many crew here on the island. What about near you?"

He heard a long sigh from Tony. "Matter of fact, it's a bit more than I thought it would be. I've been roaming around the café area, having enough caffeine to make a horse win the Derby...and I start to see lots of Chinese looking at the crew, followed by some muscle. We've got a problem. No doubt now the *Carmorra* is involved."

"Bloody hell. What now?"

"That means we've got the terrorists mixing with some other bad dudes."

"Do you want me to come back? I can get the next boat in forty minutes."

Chris heard him pause.

"Yeah, come to the vicinity of the Grambinus Café… but stay in the background. And don't call me. Text." The line went dead.

Putting his cell into his shirt pocket, Chris glanced toward Olivia. She was still listening. He sighed and walked toward the funicular and then to the docks. He felt bitter to have a peaceful afternoon interrupted. In fact, he'd experienced more than his share of bitterness lately.

I think I'm homesick.

Tony

It was nearing 6 p.m., the time smudged on the piece of paper. Tony felt himself drift out of focus. He sat in a daze rereading the text from Monica. It had been two months since she'd dumped him via phone. He slammed the cell onto the table, anger roiling up in him again.

Damn women. He'd really fallen for this Brooklyn-born Italian-American ragazza. His family liked her. He thought he'd loved her. She was a tough gal but classy. The signs were there, the drifting apart. He didn't want to be alone.

He took a sip of espresso and looked for flaws in the plans with Chris. If he didn't concentrate…all hell would break loose. The sun had almost disappeared on the Piazza del Plebiscito casting an orange glow on the faces of the people. Christopher sat at a nearby deli, wolfing down a pizza. Dusk made it difficult to distinguish features. He looked back at Chris and saw him nodding his head.

Two Chinese men strolled into the café and sat at a table in the far corner. Twenty minutes later a beefy guy with a cigar dangling from his chapped lips joined them. Tony decided to move in for a listen but stopped when two more men from the ship, crew members who'd recognize him, stumbled into the café, drunk, beer bottles raised to their lips. They took a seat in the booth behind the trio and ordered more drinks. The crew looked out of place in the elegant café.

Tony's phone beeped, and he read the text from Christopher. "Now what?"

Tony sent a message back. "U join crew. Act happy, order drink."

Tony waited to see the crew's reaction when Chris joined them. It wasn't good. Their faces deflated like punctured tires. The big guy took the winding stairs to the men's room. And one of the crew excused himself and followed.

"Crap." They were handing something off to each other. Now he'd have to wait.

Out of the corner of his eye, he saw a bright flowered shirt. Mr. Obnoxious was yelling, "Hey crew guys! Let me buy you a drink."

He sat down next to Chris and the others and ordered a round.

Chris was probably thinking the same thing as himself. "Who are these people? Are they all the bad guys?"

He had more questions than answers. But first thing on his agenda…get the scoop on the guy in the flowered shirt.

Chris nudged him. "So, I've seen you on board. I'm Chris and work as a butler in the Garden Suites."

"Hey, I'm Dick. Dick Yoder. Pleased ta meet ya. Let me buy you a drink."

"Sure, but first I need to use the restroom," said Chris.

Yoder turned and looked up the stairway. "You'll have to wait." He pointed to a sign. "The restroom is not functioning. I'm sure they'll have it fixed soon. But this is Italy. You never know." He laughed loudly and slammed Christopher on the back.

"I'll have an espresso, thank you." His cell pinged. He knew before he looked what it would say.

"Get out of there ASAP."

An hour later, the lights of the Piazza del Plebiscito illuminated families walking about on their evening *passagiatto*. Tony lost himself in the maze of handsome couples, children skipping ahead of parents, elderly women arm in arm dressed in simple but elegant attire.

Famiglia. He remembered his own Italian family in Brooklyn and sadness crept over him like a dark woolen cloak. Being employed in secret government projects left him little time for a personal life. He wondered how much longer he could live like this. Probably why Monica had dumped him. Whenever he had to leave the country, she assumed he was having an affair. And her temper? Probably wouldn't have worked out for them anyhow.

The sharp bell tone of his cell jolted him out of his reverie.

"Ciao, Chris."

"Hey, we're done for tonight. The crew left and Mr. Obnoxious is buying out the end-of-the-day pastries. His name, by the way, is Dick. I introduced myself. I'll look his name up when I get back on board. Someone put up a sign saying the restrooms were out of order. By the time I went upstairs to tag the two guys, they'd disappeared. What now?"

"Go back to the ship. We'll have dinner. My job is to uncover Mr. O's identity. He's not on our watch list. Maybe he's a loud mouth idiot, he's undercover like us, or he's in bed with these thugs."

"See you on ship. I head to crew quarters at ten. Meet again tonight?"

Tony paused, surveying the piazza. "Let's meet here in the a.m. See if you can trade with a crew member and get off. I say we arrive at six tomorrow morning to see how these guys are mixing in with the locals."

"Tony, I heard the tall blond telling her mom about a tour of Naples tomorrow. Gambrinus is high on the list of stops."

"Okay. Enjoy your evening. I hear the rum *baba'* here is better than sex. You stand by the coffee bar in the morning and listen. I'll grab a seat in the corner with a newspaper for cover."

"*Camorra* is involved. I know it."

"Don't think so, Chris. My fix is two separate things are goin' down. I meet with ship security tomorrow afternoon. We're dealing with more than terrorists. The crew is infiltrated with them...and the other stuff has to do with Naples' mafia, the Ruskies, and Chinese. Probably the Chinese MSS. Russia, not so sure. Maybe SVR."

"I'll play some pool tonight with the room stewards and see if I hear anything."

Tony snapped his cell phone and placed it on his belt hook. He waited for another swarm of people and quietly blended in until he could turn back to the ship, remaining invisible.

Dick Yoder, aka, Ivan and Russian to the bone, paid his tab and left Gambrinus, standing out like a zit on a beauty queen. He hated wearing these casual clothes and acting like a stupid American. He eyed the head steward, trying to remember his name, his eyes darting around the piazza to find the person with a cell listening to him talk. He knew there was someone undercover in the area. He spotted him at the furthest outside table. Handsome guy neatly dressed. He'd seen him on ship. He was being tailed. He needed to warn Carmella.

He covered his mouth to suppress a burp, trying to up his ante as the ugliest American in Naples. Standing out in a crowd made his job easier. His job was to recruit the poorest paid crew members to leave their jobs for what he could offer them. *It's working. They love me, they love my money.* He tugged on his flowered shirt and trudged out of the café, enjoying the disgusted stares of the upper crust Italians.

You should see me in my real clothes. Jerks.

Olivia

"Olivia, what's wrong?"

We had moved from the patio facing the main walkway of Capri to the elegant lobby inside the Quisi. Hidden in a nook behind stately potted palms, we had talked for more than two hours. He'd told me details about his life in Italy, his parents, his wife and his three children.

"I'm sorry. I just can't stop looking at you." I laughed. "It's almost too much to take in. And your English is so perfect."

"My father insisted I learn English at an early age. He knew it would be useful to me in the future." He took my hand in his. "Little did I know how much I would need it as a young man, in my business, and now with my American daughter. By the way, you also look like your grandmother. My father was from the north and favored the strong-featured people of the *Veneto*."

"I remember from the photos you sent. Will I meet the family tomorrow?"

"No. *Mi dispiace.* I am gently letting them know of your existence. It was a shock for me and will be a greater shock for them." He touched my arm. "One step at a time, Olivia. I think I must see your mother first."

I felt as though he'd slapped me.

"Why do you need to see her? She lied to me my whole life. People knew about me…my supposed father, my mother, my sister, and God only knows who else knew the secret." I pursed my lips together to hold back emotions.

"I loved your mother, Olivia. Really loved her." He stared across the bay of Naples like he could see clear to America. "We had dreams of a future."

"But…"

Mario put his finger on my lips. "I need to find out why. Why she never wrote to me, why she didn't tell me she was having my baby, why she buried this secret."

He cradled my face with his hands. "I don't expect you to understand. Just trust me." His eyes brimmed with tears.

I heaved a sigh, looked down at the table, my fingers tracing the outline of blue flowers on the linen cloth.

How could he possibly have loved my mother? Was she different then?

"I don't understand." I looked at the blue flowers again. "But I'll trust you." I hesitated. "You have to know the woman you loved doesn't exist." Resentment dripped off my words.

"Don't let her flaws control you. Move on." He took my hand in his. "I'll be here for you as long as I have breath, my dear daughter." He smiled and the room lit up for me.

He glanced at his watch. "You need to get back to the ship."

My face crumbled, tears spilling down my cheeks. "I can't leave you. Please."

"Olivia. I will be in almost every port. And when you dock in Venice, you will meet your family. You will stay with us. I promise."

I looked at him. "You say you loved Veronica. Now you say you love your wife, Angela. Which one do you love now? Did you love my mother more? Would you have married her?"

"I was young. It was a young love, exciting. I never forgot her, but I assure you Angela is the very heart and soul of me."

We walked arm in arm to the *funicular*. The lights in the harbor twinkled while we descended the cliffs toward the port and the now black sea. The last boat was loading for Naples. We hugged tightly. Mario placed a cell phone in my hand.

"For you. Use this to call me. It's set up with my cell and is only for us to call each other. I'll see you in Florence. And we will tell your mother that day. *Ti amo, Olivia. Ti voglio bene!*"

I boarded the boat without looking back. My father's repeated "I love you" enclosed me like a security blanket. I would share dinner with my mother and Ashley and rave about Capri. Lie? Sure, I would lie just like my mother. No problem.

Who on earth was this "woman" my father had loved? Was I the reason she started drinking? Was it guilt over an affair?

But in the back of my mind, I remembered Ashley's story of Mother, dressed to perfection, always with a drink in her manicured hand.

I made it back to the ship at seven p.m.. The gangplank was heavily guarded since it was available all night. The ship wouldn't leave until noon tomorrow. No way could I face dinner with my mother and sister. Couldn't do it. My stomach had been doing more flips than an Olympic gymnast. My mother was the last person I wanted to see.

A staff member greeted me when I swiped my ship card to board.

"Where's the casino?"

"Fourth deck mid-ship. But it's closed while we're in port. Opens tomorrow an hour after we leave Naples. About one p.m."

"Thanks." I flashed a smile of appreciation and walked toward the stairs. Figured walking up two flights was better than being crammed into an elevator with cruisers. I felt both elated and angry.

I felt a tap on my shoulder. "So you didn't go to dinner, either?"

"Tony, hi! Nope. But I hear there are some great restaurants on board this ship." He took my hand. "Come on, I'm buying."

"I'm not hungry, but a drink would be nice."

"Let's head to the top of the ship and see what happens." He grinned.

"I need to drop some things off in my room. Come with me and we'll go from there." A few minutes later we strolled into my suite. I held my breath hoping my mom and sister were still in the dining room.

The butler was turning down my bed.

"Hi, Christopher. Did you have a busy day?"

"Very, Miss Olivia. And you?"

"Had a fabulous day on Capri."

I thought I noticed a subtle eye contact between him and Tony.

"Sir, I'm doing your room next. Any requests?'

"As a matter of fact, I do want to give you some things I need pressed for formal night." He turned to me. "Sorry for the delay. Meet me in the observation lounge. I'll be there in ten minutes. Order us the drink of the day." He touched the tip of my nose.

"Come on, Christopher," he said. "Let me fetch the clothes I need washed and pressed."

The minute Tony opened his door, Christopher erupted. "Are you nuts? What if she suspects something?" He leaned against the closed door of Tony's suite.

"You looked like you had information," said Tony. "You were sending me strong signals."

"Well, I do have info. That wacky tourist with the loud mouth? He's Russian."

"Russian? You're kidding me, right? He's more American than me. No accent." Tony leaned in to Christopher. "Why do you say that?"

"I saw him on a cell phone and, for once, he spoke softly. Made me suspicious. So I edged close to him. He was speaking bloody Russian, and he was angry. That's why I made a point of speaking with him and introducing myself. Not a trace of accent. He's good."

Tony pounded the wall. "Could this get any more complicated? If he's a Ruskie, then he's tied in with the Camorra."

He paced across the dimly lit carpet, stopped, looked at Chris and said, "We've got terrorists from the Philippines, and Russians and Chinese connecting with the Naples mafia, and a female bartender handing off notes to both. What the hell?"

"Better not keep your date waiting, Tony."

"She's not my date. Just another woman."

Chris threw his hands in the air. "What chick made you so bitter about the fairer sex?" He opened the door and walked away, mumbling.

Tony took out his cell and called his handler.

"Yeah?"

"We've got problems, Sir. Lots of them. That flower-shirted guy we've been tailing? He's Russian."

The gruff voice on the other end ordered him to a meeting. "Two hours, my room. And make a point to talk to this so-called Russian yourself."

Tony made his way to the elevator to meet Olivia. He wanted nothing more at that moment than a warm bed and a warm body. He sighed. A strong stomach-warming drink would have to do.

Olivia

The lounge at the ship's bow was a popular after-dinner night spot for older passengers, those who'd lived in the big band era. Dim lighting, music, soft leather chairs, and spectacular views. It was romantic and invited intimacy. Since the ship was docked overnight, the place was quieter than usual. The lights of Naples beckoned.

Tony and I were seated at a cozy table for two in the darkest corner of the lounge as far away from the band as possible.

"So what did you enjoy the most about Capri today?" Tony asked, touching my arm.

"Everything. It was probably the most beautiful water I've ever seen."

"Olivia!"

Tony flinched and sank back into his chair.

Ashley rushed toward us, mother in tow. Mom wore her I'm-ready-for-an-argument-face normally resulting from too much alcohol. What had my father seen in her? Both of them, the one who raised me and Mario.

"You lied to us, Olivia." My mother's face was crinkled with anger.

"Calm down, Mother," said Ashley. She took Mom's hand and pulled her close.

"What are you talking about?" I asked, feigning ignorance.

"Someone saw you in Capri with a handsome man. Said you were holding hands and kissing." Mom stood stiff, pulled away from Ash and jammed her hands onto her hips. "You have some explaining to do. What a trampy thing, to run off with a perfect stranger from a ship and avoid being with your sister and me? I raised you better than that." She took a deep breath. "And now we find you here with this man all over you."

You should know all about trampy, Mother. And who on earth would tell her about me meeting a man on the Island of Capri? Nosey passengers passing by, just making a mention of it to her? Doesn't matter.

I stood up, looked at my mother, and said with deadly calm, "I'm a grown woman. Back off." I turned to Tony. "I'm so sorry. I'm going to my room now. Since we need to be on board by noon tomorrow, why don't we meet for lunch? Call me in the morning." I leaned down, took his face in my hands, and kissed him until neither of us could breathe.

That ought to get her.

I pivoted and strode toward the doorway, leaving everyone staring at me. When the elevator door closed, I buried my face in my hands, muffling a scream. Every repressed bit of anger toward my mom surfaced like an erupting volcano. I ran from the elevator to my room, locked the door, threw myself on my bed and cried into a pillow, pounding the bed with rage that surprised me.

Tony

Tony stood rock still, shocked by the kiss, and Olivia's exit. That kiss had damn near turned him inside out. When able to move, he nodded goodnight to Ashley and Veronica and hurried to the exit before erupting into laughter. The look on the faces of the perfect sister and her obviously sloshed mother! He punched the sixth- deck button to meet his boss as promised. He touched his mouth and smiled.

He knocked on the cabin door.

Joe opened the door, picked up his drink in one hand and holstered his gun. "Get in here. And wipe the damn lipstick off your face. We've got a huge problem."

Tony noticed the clenched jaw of his handler and the stare of the glacial eyes. "That loudmouth you've been following? He's Russian mafia, on board with a false passport as Dick Yoder from Parsippany, New Jersey. Actually, he's here to recruit disgruntled crew into the fashion business to work in Italy for twice the money. In the sweat shops. I ran his passport photo through our computer. His real name is Ivan Zozlow, and he's high on Interpol's list."

"So help me out, here, Joe. The Ruskies are going to pay the crew a living wage and you're angry about that? Do you know how much these Filipinos make a month and how long they're gone from their family?" Tony moved towards the wine bottle on the bar, paused, and shrugged. "I'm not getting it. I thought we were on board to try to uncover crew or whoever is spreading the virus on this ship. Who the hell are the bad guys at this point?"

In a deadly tone, Joe said, "Let's talk about the good guys first. Poor Filipinos, away from their families, breaking off to join the Russian Mafia…who are connected to the *Camorra* in Naples and the Chinese Mafia? Are you freakin' kidding me?"

He paced, slammed his gun on the bar and slugged back a full glass of wine. "These Filipinos will be required to deliver drugs, drug money, carry out assassination orders, live in dirty flats in the heart of Naples, work in sweat shops for the fashion industry, and other things you cannot even imagine."

Tony stiffened at each word.

"You have no idea how much more difficult our job just became." Joe kept glaring at Tony. "In fact," Joe lumbered toward his gun, "let's take a few minutes to see how the 'poor Filipino crew' live on this ship." He fetched his cell from his side pants pocket and punched in some numbers.

"Hey, Joe Tucci here. Need to wander around the crew area for about thirty minutes. Meet me there in ten."

"Follow me, Tony," he said, holstering his gun inside his jacket.

Ten minutes later, Tony and his handler entered the crew lounge. Tony felt as though he'd stepped into a fantasy world. Immediate impressions were of a large entertainment area. The crack of pool balls smacked over the laughter of the crew in casual clothes enjoying table games. An internet center of thirty or forty computers lined the right wall. Music blared from Bose speakers. The bar was lined with workers, clinking glasses and chatting.

Tony heard a plethora of languages mixed in with broken English, most of which he recognized, some he didn't.

"Come on," said Joe, hi-fiving crew while he led Tony into the cafeteria.

"Enzo," he shouted to one of the chefs. "Want to introduce you to my friend, here."

Tony shook Enzo's hand.

"Enzo is in charge of the kitchen crew." Joe waved his hands toward the amazing display of salads, fruit, meat-carving stations, and beverages. "Still think the poor crew would be better off with the mob? They eat as well as the guests on board this vessel, have karaoke every night, entertainers, the best music, crew to wait on them…yeah, that's right. Crew for the crew." He slapped Tony on the back. "Want to see more?"

Tony shook his head. "This is like another ship down here."

"Yes, it is. Sixty-five different nationalities represented, for the most part a big family. All required to speak English. Relaxing. Smiling. Come on. I'll show you the library."

At one in the morning, Tony returned to his room, puzzled and exhausted. He understood. Undoing his tie, he reached with his left hand into the refrigerator and pulled out a diet soda, then opened the slider and strolled to the railing. He was thankful the ship was docked overnight. The sea was rough sending white foam crashing against the side of the ship. The waves were awash in light from the decks of the vessel. The air surrounded him with its fresh scent. He leaned out further, thinking about the twelve hundred crew members on deck three, the ones who served him and the lucky passengers on the ship, far from home, lonely, yet bonded in a way he found puzzling.

Tony thought about the human side he'd seen of his handler…almost jolly with the crew. He seldom saw him smile. Joe communicated with a cold and steady tone of voice and his intense glacier blue eyes. Tony inhaled deeply hoping the fresh salty air off the coast of Naples would clear his head. Leaning his forehead onto the rail, he made his decision. Not on his watch. Not one person working on The Pearl would be sucked into the pig's trough known as mafia…be they Italian, Russian, or Chinese. The crew quarters may appear state of the art, but in reality, there was no place like home. And these young people still worked for nothing, worked like slaves. The Russians wouldn't make it any better for them; in fact, the conditions would be worse.

Day Three – Second Day
In Port Of Naples
Olivia

The morning Mediterranean sparkled, cobalt blue, dancing diamonds flashing with intolerable brightness. The lapping of water against the ship eased me into relaxation despite my pensive mood. The sting of salty air cleared my mind.

Leaning against the mahogany veranda rail, I stared broodingly at the sea, trying to remember my early childhood. My mother's outburst in front of Tony last night had embarrassed me. It brought shadowed memories of me as a small child, always cringing when my mother called.

I sipped my coffee and took a bite of the roll my butler had delivered earlier. Nothing tasted right, the coffee seemed bitter, and my eyes were still puffy from last night's hysterical crying. I hoped Mom and Ash hadn't heard me, but, then again…I hoped they felt miserable. Fat chance.

For the first time in many months, hatred churned inside as I thought of my ex and how he'd ruined my life. If not for him, I'd still have a part-time teaching job, I'd be in my lovely home, entertaining friends, reading, maybe taking a few laps in our pool. But, no. Here I was on a different continent, my loony-toon sister's idea of a final trip with "Mom" turning out to be a nightmare. Ashley was so sure this would be a wonderful healing experience for us before my mother met her maker. And after last night, I truly hoped she'd meet Him soon.

Think about Mario. Only Mario. Okay, Tony, too.

Peeking around the corner of the balcony onto the main veranda, I observed Ashley and mom drinking coffee at the table, staring daggers at each other. I knew Ashley was thinking how to fix everything between me and "the mom."

Taking a deep breath, I squared my shoulders and leaned over the rail with a yell. "Mind if I join you for breakfast? Beautiful morning, huh?"

Ashley waved to me and said a bit too brightly, "Oh, Olivia, dear. We've been hoping you'd wake up. We ordered a wonderful breakfast. Fresh fruit and rolls and cappuccinos."

"Be there in a minute. Need to put on my robe."

I wondered if I should go for the kill and broach the subject of my real father. Or should I take it slow, and sneak it in a little at a time?

With a sigh, I donned my gauze yellow robe, slipped into my white sandals, and opened my door onto the deck at the top of this lovely ship, wondering how such a setting had turned into a pressure cooker.

"Good morning," I said, trying not to clench my teeth.

"Dear, come and sit next to me." Mother patted the chair.

"I don't want to face the sun." I pulled the chair out across from her.

"So, Olivia, isn't this just the perfect day? Look at this view, our own private hideaway from the other two-thousand people on board."

"Actually, I like being with new people. I'm probably going to play Trivia today and go to the spa for a massage. Then–" I smiled, hoping it was dazzling– "I have a date for lunch."

Couldn't help myself. I had to start the day being ornery.

"About that." Ashley took her three-hundred-dollar Prada shades from her face and looked directly at me, placing her soft manicured hand onto mine. "Mom is sorry about last night." She turned to the feeble Veronica. "Aren't you sorry, Mom?"

Mom leaned onto the table with her elbows and smiled. But her eyes weren't smiling. "I really was out of line last night. Too many drinks."

No kidding, Sherlock.

"Forget about it. But, Mom, you shouldn't drink while you still have chemo in your system."

She looked down. "I know," she said, her voice soft.

"I have a question for you, Mom."

She looked at me, a brief shadow crossing her face. "Do we have to have questions now? Before breakfast?"

The ding of the elevator announced an arrival, Christopher carrying a vase with a single yellow rose.

"For you, Ma'am." He bowed.

I took the card from the stem.

Meet me at Trivia. We'll do lunch. Tony

I folded the note in my hand, pushed my chair back and said, "See you around the ship. I have a date at the morning Trivia game." Without another word, I sashayed into my room, a wild smile on my face. Not because I had a lunch date with Tony. But because I had left them speechless. Yes, it was going to be a good day.

Tony

Tony's body fell limp on the balcony chaise. He stared blankly into the marmalade sunrise burning off the haze hovering over the Bay of Naples, remembering Olivia's kiss.

He reached for a glass of orange juice on the small white table to his right.

His phone sang a familiar aria from La Traviata, jolting him out of his daydream of spending a day with Olivia.

"Good morning, Sir. Your dry cleaning is being delivered."

"But…" The phone went dead, followed by the buzz of the doorbell to his suite…three quick buzzes.

He charged to the door, mildly irritated at the interruption of his thoughts of Olivia, and opened it to his butler, Christopher.

"Good morning, sir." He bowed and strode directly to the closet, freshly bagged suit in hand. He lowered his voice. "We need to talk. Two more people are near death from the so-called "noro virus.""

Tony strained to hear. "Quit speaking to the suit," he said.

Chris nodded toward the secure second bedroom. Tony grabbed the sweeping device from the safe in his closet. With the door closed, they scoured the room with the sweeper, powered down the computer and removed the batteries from the cell phones.

"Clear," said Tony.

"Room's clean," said Chris. "Now we need to talk."

They sat in the chairs near the desk and stared at each other for a moment.

"Security and the ship's doc are more than concerned. If more people get sick, or die, ports won't let us dock." Chris's forehead wrinkled in frustration.

"What the heck? The whole reason for this undercover op is supposed to be about crew possibly being a part of a terror plot involving a virus. Now we discover some of the crew are jumping ship and organizing with different bad guys."

"I know," said Chris. "But we discovered something else yesterday. Still have to check that out. But get this. We think one of the crew may be carrying a virus. Think about it. With two-thirds of the people on this ship American, they could wipe out a lot of people and it would take forever to learn the truth." He paused a moment, out of breath. "We've also stumbled into an operation for the Camorra. They're recruiting for the fashion industry, promising more money and a better life. The Chinese and the Russians are in on it."

"Have you lost your secret-undercover-mind?" Tony combed his fingers through his hair and glowered. "I was given an undercover operation to find out one thing. Is there a plot, sponsored by terrorists, to take down a cruise ship? Now you're telling me to change all that? And what about the boss? He hasn't discussed any other options with me."

Tony leaned back in his chair, frowning. "What the heck was the big show last night for? You know, the crew quarters, showing me how great their life was, why no one would want to leave…" He waved his hand in the air. "Not to mention they work six days a week, ten hours a day, and are away from their families for six to eight months at a time. Who'd want to give up that life?" He shrugged, a fake smile on his face.

"Your handler will contact you tonight after dinner at the disco party on the lido deck. Lots of people, loud music, every server and busboy will be on deck. We have our guys in the crew quarters doing some digging on computers. It will be a perfect time to see who is connected to what."

Tony puffed out a loud sigh of frustration. "Pull up the information we've gathered on this."

Turning the computer on, Chris went into geek mode, glancing now and then at Tony, feeling the heat from his glare.

Tony watched, frustrated. "So much for my date with Olivia." He pounded the desk. "*I hate this job.*"

He picked up his phone, dialed Olivia's cell and got her answering service. "Olivia, I'm so sorry. I had some work-related emails come in this morning. Probably won't see you until dinner. Hope you like the flower." He snapped the phone shut, took his contact phone and called his handler, Joe.

Joe answered gruffly. "I'm on the crowd at Gambrinus. You can thank me for taking over your detail and letting you sleep."

"Thank you, sir. But I have a very strong hunch this mission is all for nothing. I'm not being paid to follow Russians and Chinese."

"You're being paid by NeroMare, and we'll follow the leads until someone tells us to stop. Now do your job."

Tony heard the phone buzz, ending the conversation. He massaged his shoulders, trying to ease the constant tension that came with this assignment.

Olivia

I looked at the note from Tony, disappointment flooding me. No Trivia date. I went by myself and sat with an already formed group. They were a group of five ladies from Canada who enthusiastically welcomed me, telling me I could help with questions dealing with the United States.

Sally patted me on the knee. "We're all good at this. And our strength is questions about the United Kingdom and Europe. Glad to have you with us."

We won the game answering an impressive nineteen out of twenty questions. The grand prize was a luggage tag for each of us.

Since I no longer had a lunch date, I made my way to the poolside grill for a slice of pizza, hoping to avoid any personal contact with my family. At noon, the ship glided out of the Port of Naples, and I listened to the band play. At one o'clock on the dot, the cruise director announced the casino was open. I made my way to the elevator and hit the button for the fourth floor.

I heard the casino before I saw it.

I stomped into the garish smoke-filled room and looked for a slot machine isolated from the big tables. Bells rang everywhere. Smokers had already created a blue haze, making the pink, purple and gold blend into one giant kaleidoscope of color.

I spotted some quarter machines along the wall, sat at the end. It was a Pink Panther Machine that played the theme song over and over. I popped in a twenty and started the game. It was mesmerizing. The silly panther ran back and forth across the screen with the inspector close behind. My twenty edged up to one hundred. I was hooked. I pulled the lever again. "Come on, Panther. Come on!"

Ding, ding, ding, ding. The sound of quarters tumbling into the tray. It wouldn't stop. I looked up and saw the white light on top whirling like a lighthouse beam.

A bleached blonde, tight-faced woman two machines down started to scream. "You won. Wow! Oh my gosh. You hit the jackpot."

I peered at the screen. The goofy and addictive Pink Panther song continued to play over the clang of falling coins. The Panther ran all over the screen, smiling cagily and making faces at a prone and shocked inspector.

A small crowd started to gather, making me uncomfortable. I'd come here to hide, after all.

A slightly built man approached holding a chain laden with keys. "Looks like this is your lucky day." His accent was thick 'Down Under Aussie.' "Congratulations, ducky. You just won yourself four- thousand dollars."

"Huh?" *Did he say I won four-thousand dollars?*

The casino manager kept talking, instructing me where to sign on the white piece of paper he'd placed in front of me. "Take this to the Cashier to get your money. And here's a bag of souvenirs."

"Some people are just lucky. In your case beautiful and lucky."

I turned and my eyes gazed into the chocolate eyes of Tony. The stomach gymnastics started again.

"May I help you spend your money?" He grinned.

"I thought you weren't available until after dinner?" I was so happy to see him I could have jumped up and hugged him. "What are you doing here? How did you find me?"

Tony smiled. "My meeting was interrupted; I was feeling out of sorts and decided to walk around the ship. Went to the running deck and looked down at the pool. Saw you disappear to the elevator."

"And…?"

"I tried the library, the coffee shop, and the casino." He shrugged his shoulders. "Heard someone scream and the dinging and here I am." He leaned in for a kiss. "I seem to always find you, Olivia."

"Do you have to return to your meeting?" I smiled, hopeful.

"Afraid so. But I'll make it a point to see you after dinner." He squeezed my shoulders and with a sigh, walked away.

My sigh echoed his. Guess I had no excuse to avoid dinner with my family.

Day Four - Port Of Livorno
Gateway to Florence and Tuscany
Olivia

The text from Mario last night had been straight-forward. "Meet me at Argenteria SACCHI, two bridges down from the Pontevecchio. Just before Santa Trinita. It's marked on the map I gave you. Mario."

The port of Livorno was a huge disappointment, a typical shipyard full of containers and noisy equipment. Nothing but concrete and steel. But it was the main port for the ship to deliver passengers to Tuscan wine country, Florence, and the still-leaning Tower of Pisa. The number of buses waiting to transport us for various tours was dizzying. And, although I hated buses, relief flooded me when we finally settled onto Tour Bus 104, appropriately named "Florence on Your Own." This meant we'd be herded to a designated spot on the river Arno along with hundreds of other escorted tourists and left to wander.

Ashley and Mother wanted to shop. They had no interest in museums or "The David," when the smell of Italian leather filled the air, not to mention Italian gold. I knew I could escape from the endless shops by buying a ticket for L'Academia and David. Hopefully, I wouldn't see Ash and Mom again until we returned to the bus. Yesterday morning's brief "Tour of Old Naples" had felt rushed. I hadn't wanted to go, but Tony's call had set me free, and Ashley insisted I do the tour with them. Today, I wanted nothing to do with a tour or shopping. I just wanted to see my father.

"You're moody. What's your problem?" Ashley asked, her tone condescending.

"I'm fine. Just tired is all." I smiled like a Miss Universe contestant, tilting my head toward them. "Mostly I'm excited to see David. And his backside."

"Honestly, Olivia," said Mom. "You can be so crude. Like you want to shock me or hurt my feelings."

Mom's whining irritated me. But I continued to smile. "Mom, David's other side? Come on. Everyone wants to see all of David." I laughed, trying to lighten the mood.

Ashley smiled. "You see David; we'll see gold and leather." She patted Mom's arm and looked out the window.

I edged closer to my window, watched the city disappear and the hills of Tuscany swell with groves of olive trees and vineyards, and I thought of Mario. My plan: to find out what he meant by my mother being so special. I glanced at her, small and frail, a sympathetic figure at this time to be sure. But her face showed lines of bitterness and a hard life. Her choice. I swung between anger, resentment, and pure pity for her. Love? Hard to muster. But she was my mother. I leaned my head against the bus window and sighed.

As I suspected, the bus stopped an hour later at a point just north of the city center. Florence had not allowed automobiles or buses of any kind into the city for many years due to the pollution of the buildings and art. The line of buses seemed unending.

When the driver opened the door, a slim young lady in a milk-chocolate brown suit enhanced by a gorgeous scarf of deep teals and gold, jumped on board with her leather boots and smiled. A waft of bus fumes followed her.

"*Buon giorno*. I am Ludovica. I will show you where we will meet at five this afternoon. Please follow me in a single line." She held a sad bouquet of artificial sunflowers high over her head. "*Andiamo.*"

We lined up like schoolchildren trying not to lose track of her. There were dozens of similar flower bouquets and umbrellas being waved by tour guides. The walk took about ten minutes.

"This is the Piazza Santa Croce. There on the steps of the church you will wait for me at five." She pointed to a shop on the corner. "That coffee bar will allow you to use the restroom if you buy a coffee or water. I have maps for each of you with recommendations for eating and shopping." She reached into her satchel and pulled out rubber-banded maps and handed them to us as we passed by.

The grandeur of Florence was momentarily obscured while we fought the throngs of people. It seemed as though every inch of air swelled with clumps of tourists.

Mom clutched Ashley by the arm while they weaved through the crowds. I followed.

"This is ridiculous," said Ashley, holding her purse tightly to her chest. "So where do you want to meet after your museum visits?"

"You know, I really don't want to rush through any of them. Would you mind if we just met for coffee like at – oh – maybe two? We can meet at the end of the Pontevecchio. You know me and art." Again I plastered on the fake beauty queen smile.

"Whatever." Ashley shrugged and forged ahead, Mom hanging onto her arm.

I waited until they were out of sight, swallowed by the crowds, and ambled to the river wall to check out my map. The one from Mario. The sidewalk by the Arno River emptied once I passed by the old bridge. The sun had broken through the clouds giving way to a bit of blue in the muddied Arno waters. Across the river, villas dotted the rolling hills, pine trees swayed. My heart and soul focused not on the city's beauty, but on seeing the gentle face of my father. It was eleven when I arrived at *Argenteria Sacchi*, a beautiful jewelry store tucked under a blue canopy, the windows filled with jewels and silver. The bell chimed at the opening of the door. And there stood Mario, his bronzed face beaming.

"Mia figlia bella." His hug was fierce, as though I might vanish. "I have a gift for you." He reached to the counter and picked up a deep blue box bound with yellow ribbon.

I opened it to find a charm bracelet unlike any I'd seen. The small sterling silver squares were filled with scenes of Italy, historic landmarks like the Coliseum. One square held the Italian flag, another a passport, and the center charm was embellished with a diamond under which was engraved the word, 'Papa'. The final charm had been engraved with my name.

I stood, overcome with emotion, unable to speak, tears threatening to spill. A piece of jewelry from a father was special.

"Andiamo, Olivia. Let's have lunch and talk about your mother."

I tensed for a moment, then took his offered arm and walked down the street and around a corner to a tiny restaurant in an alley. *Trattoria Garga*. The name forever imprinted on my mind as the place where I would hear about the mother I'd never met.

The restaurant was fragrant with rosemary, tomato sauce, garlic, and cheese, and the earthy tang of wine. The brightly colored walls and murals showed scenes of the Tuscan hills and olive groves. Opera blared from the speakers, pots and pans banged, and singing waiters hurried from the kitchen to tables. The place was brimming with locals. And the Italian language hummed pleasantly, keeping me firmly placed in Italy. No tourists meant no ship people.

Mario asked for a table in the far corner.

An hour later, after some local wine to loosen my lips, and the best food I'd tasted in a long time, I was ready to stop the talk about Mario's family and ask some questions about Veronica.

"Tell me, Mario." I licked a bit of tomato sauce dripping down my chin. "What was Veronica like when you met her?"

He straightened in his chair, a faraway look in his eyes and sighed. He signaled to a waiter to bring him an espresso. "Please, call me Papa'." Leaning forward, he began.

"She was an angel in white. Tall and thin, hair so golden it took my breath away. Eyes blue, deep blue like a glacier, a straight patrician nose, lips thick with natural redness. She wore a simple white dress hugging her figure, no jewelry. A vision.

She was sitting in the lobby of the Biltmore hotel. I'd gone to meet an ambassador from Italy who was visiting the embassy in Los Angeles. We both noticed her. But she captured my heart at once. Young and away from home for the first time." He shrugged in frustration.

I struggled to remember her when I was a kid. I'd seen old photos and knew she'd been a beauty. But my so-called dad had been like a Norwegian god, tall and striking with his light skin, light hair and piercing blue eyes always filled with humor. My mom's eyes always seemed bitter in contrast. Almost like she'd expected more from him than he could give.

"Olivia, you're not listening." Mario tapped me on the arm. "I smiled at her, and when she returned the smile, I was lost. I came back to the hotel several times hoping to find her. Weeks later, I wandered into the softly lit bar of the Biltmore. She was sitting at a corner table next to a gilded statue looking lonely, pensive. Taking a deep breath, I gathered courage to approach her. She was drinking wine the color of her hair, her long fingers curled around the stem of the glass. Her head nodded to the chair next to her.

"My name is Veronica." Her voice was low and breathy.

I responded. "I am Mario. I hoped I would see you again."

"And for the next week, we met every day. She enchanted me. I was lonely, in a strange country. By the second week, we were lovers."

My eyebrows rose. "But she was married. Did you know that?"

"Yes. And I was promised to someone in Italy. I was reckless, guilty, and ashamed, yet I kept seeing her." He looked down, paused. When his eyes met mine, they glittered with tears.

He stopped talking when the waiter delivered his coffee. He held the small cup in his hand, drank it, and said, "I've never loved another woman the same. I love my Angelina very much, but not in the same way. My love for my wife is pure and lasting. My love for Veronica brought thrills and excitement…a forbidden love. And I never knew you existed because my letters to Veronica came back as undeliverable. Only your determination to find me has reunited us."

He stopped speaking. The silence cut into me. He took my hands in his. "I should have rescued her. Saved her from that monster she was married to. But I didn't. It has been the regret of my life."

Rescued her from a monster? The room blurred and spun. My chest tightened as though it held a great weight. I found it difficult to breathe.

"Olivia? Are you okay?"

I felt frozen. Mario took my face in his hands. "Olivia?"

"Papa', has my whole life been a lie, a sham? My 'father' a monster? My mother an angel? I don't understand." My hands curled into fists.

Mario looked down and sighed.

I wondered if he had told his sweet Angela about me.

A thought flashed through my mind. I asked him, "Mario, not only was Veronica married, she was ten years older than you? I'm sorry. This whole situation is so convoluted to me. And you keep saying how special Veronica was, yet you say you love your wife, yet you never forgot Veronica."

"My dear Olivia, you have been unlucky in love, right? You know the challenges of the heart. Have patience. The only thing that matters now is we've found each other, and we all need to make peace and ask forgiveness. I promise you, all will be okay. Please trust me."

"I'll try. I do trust you, but don't understand so much."

We hugged each other goodbye, with Mario promising he'd make everything clear and right with me. I felt nothing but confusion. I turned to wave again. He stood watching me. I slowly walked toward the Piazza Santa Croce meeting place for our bus, dreading the questions I knew would be forthcoming from my mother and sister. I wondered if they'd tried to meet me at two? I'd hear about it if they did.

Fortunately, they were able to board the bus first. I hung back and climbed in at the second door, remembering the conversation with my father, gazing at the bracelet he'd given me.

When the bus arrived at the ship, I knew I needed time alone.

"Mom, Ash, I am really tired. Didn't sleep well last night, and my feet hurt from all the walking. Would you mind if I go to my room and take a nap?"

"Of course not, dear," Mom said. "I'm going to do the same thing. Go right to bed." She turned to Ashley. "And you, sweetheart?"

"I'm meeting Anders for the wine tasting before dinner. Going to freshen up first." She glanced at my wrist. "Lovely bracelet, Olivia. Good for you. I'm glad you treated yourself to something special from Italy."

"Yeah. Couldn't resist it. Unusual, right?"

I sighed with relief as we made our way up the gang-plank. We pushed the button for the elevator, rode up without speaking, and entered the suite.

"See you later," I said, closing my door. I sat on my bed my head filled with emotion from all the information of the day. No resolution and more confusion.

Sea Day – Day Five
Veronica

Veronica sighed with relief to be left alone on the deck. She knew Olivia and Ashley were concerned. She was glad her daughters were busy having fun. Today, however, she needed to be alone. Her heart was pounding from the fear of death.

Despite the afternoon heat hammering onto the open deck in front of her bedroom, Veronica huddled on the deck chair under the duvet from her bed, shivering from the damp sea air and trying to ignore her illness. She felt nothing but gratefulness it was a sea day, with no difficult ports to navigate.

Her body punished her constantly with pain. Time was short. She wanted to confront and confess and make things right with her girls. She rolled the amber plastic bottle in her hand. Could she do it?

She picked up the bottle of Chardonnay and poured the amber wine into her glass, filling it to the top. She sipped the wine slowly at first, then swallowed large gulps.

Her eyes felt heavy. The bottle slipped from her limp hand, and her wine-hazed sleep transported her back in time.

"Eric? Is that you?"

Veronica smoothed her satin sapphire dress, the material outlining her slim figure. She slipped into her nude heels and leaned into the mirror, putting the recent gift of diamond studs in her ears.

"I'll be perfect for Eric," she whispered to her image in the full-length mirror. "Tonight we'll make another baby."

The doorbell rang. She ran downstairs to greet the sitter.

"Gosh, Mrs. Andersen, you look fabulous." Maryann smiled. "Anything special you want me to do for Ashley tonight?"

"Thanks. No. Nothing special. Ashley's already in bed. Feel free to go to sleep in the upstairs den. We'll be late tonight."

She closed the front door, her heart racing, and walked to her sleek black Beamer. Sliding behind the wheel, she rested her head on the back of the seat and prayed. "Please, God. Eric must love me tonight."

Without remembering the drive or how she arrived, she pulled up to a valet at the front of the famous Beverly Hills

Hotel. A young man in a black suit with lapels trimmed in red rushed to open her door and took her hand to assist her.

"My name is Ron. I'll take excellent care of your car."

"Thank you," she said. "Here are the keys. My name is Veronica Andersen."

The Hollywood Ballroom was the largest and furthest away. Veronica trembled with anticipation. She spotted Eric immediately. His blond hair and chiseled features were enhanced by the black tuxedo. Standing a head taller than anyone around him, he was, as usual, the focus of attention. She noted a dark-haired woman who seemed to be leaning against his arm with her hand resting a bit too possessively on his hand. The other hand held a drink. Veronica hung back for a moment, composing herself, and tried to quell the million butterflies battling for space in her stomach. She straightened, swung her long golden hair and walked toward Eric with a brilliant smile.

"Eric. You should wear a tuxedo all the time." She reached up to kiss him on the cheek.

Eric drew back. "Vronny, careful of my drink." He smiled at her, but his lips were tight and Veronica knew he was displeased at her bold entrance. He preferred her to be in the background, soft, quiet, and beautiful…an extension of him, but a silent one. His agitation made her nervous. It became more obvious he was avoiding her as the evening wore on. He looked away from her when she tried to catch his eye. He left her alone for long periods of time and constantly had his arms around other women.

The night lumbered along with meaningless dinner conversation, phony laughter, and a single dance with her husband. Eric was a graceful dancer. She knew they made an impression on the dance floor.

But Veronica felt no joy inside. She observed the servers continually filling Eric's wine glass and knew he was drinking more than he realized. She observed his flirtations, his flattery, his charm, laying the foundations of business for his real estate kingdom.

When she thought she couldn't tolerate another minute pretending to be happy, Eric approached her, held her arm a bit too tight, and announced it was time to go home. He leaned in to give her a kiss on the cheek, and whispered, "Smile, woman. For God's sake, smile."

With a wave to the partiers hanging on until the last moment, they smiled. Eric again grabbed her arm, squeezing painfully, and they walked in silence to the valet desk.

"Which car did you bring?" asked Eric.

"The Beamer," she said, nodding to the valet.

The ride home was quiet, filled with tension. She rested her hand on his thigh and leaned her head on his shoulder, hoping to signal her need for him tonight. While Eric paid the sitter, Veronica rushed to her room and slipped into her new gown of pale yellow, added a subtle spray of his favorite Chanel perfume and waited for him. The satin felt soft on her skin. She'd paid so much money for this gown at the Bullock's in downtown Los Angeles.

He walked into the bedroom grumbling about a sale he almost had and ripped off his tux, piece by piece, throwing it on the floor. "I'm exhausted."

Veronica hugged him from behind and kissed his back, stroking his stomach. "I want to make love," she whispered.

He pulled the straps from her shoulders, his hands clumsy. After the gown dropped to the floor, she stood naked. He bent down, picked up the garment and tossed it into the corner.

Veronica moved closer to him, rubbing her breasts against his chest.

He shoved her away. "I told you. I'm tired." His voice slurred from the alcohol.

"Eric, I love you. I want to make love." She reached her hands to his face and stood on her tiptoes to kiss him.

"Let's get it done, then," he said, pulling her onto the bed, his breath reeking of wine and stale cigar.

The lovemaking was hurried and unfulfilling. When Eric couldn't perform, a knot of fear pulled at her stomach and tears filled her eyes blurring Eric's angry face.

"It's okay, sweetheart," she said. "Just hold me."

That was the moment he slapped her face.

She inhaled sharply.

"You're the reason I can't perform. You always have to be in control." He rolled onto his back next to her, panting. "I never feel like a man with you. You're too damned needy." He closed his eyes and passed out from too much alcohol.

Veronica clenched her fists and wondered if she'd made a mistake in her marriage. Wondering if Eric was right. If it was her fault.

She lay there, quiet tears streaming down her face, and waited for the natural rhythm of his sleep. She slipped from the bed and wandered into her little girl's room. She watched Ashley's sweet face lost in an innocent sleep, crawled into the bed and curled into a ball next to her. Spilling tears, she shut down every shred of love, and every positive emotion she'd ever felt for her husband.

Veronica heard footsteps and her eyes popped open. At first she was puzzled at her surroundings and then realized she'd been dreaming. Her dream had been so real and she breathed a sigh of relief to remember she was on a ship and Eric was dead. She reached for her glass of wine.

Ashley walked across the deck to tell her mom where she was going and saw her slumped on the deck chair.

"Mother, what's wrong?" Ashley leaned into Veronica, brushing the stray hair from her forehead. "You're shaking." She peered closer, sheltering her eyes from the sun. "And you're crying? Are you in pain?"

Veronica brushed away her tears, angry at herself for crying over that fool. "Oh, for goodness sake, quit hovering over me. I'm fine. Just enjoying the sea day and the sun." Veronica shook her head to steady her thoughts. She wasn't ready to tell Ashley the truth about her father. Not yet.

" Anders has asked me to join him for lunch and invited you and Olivia. Want to come with us?"

"No, thanks, Ash. I just want to sit here and be quiet."

"Have you eaten anything today?"

"I'm not really hungry, dear."

"You have to eat. I'll send Christopher up with some fresh fruit and cheese. You need some protein."

Veronica reached for her daughter's hand. "I'm okay, really. Just want to be alone for awhile." She drew her hand away. "The port days have worn me down."

"Okay. I'll take your word for it." Ashley paused a moment, sighed, and walked to the phone to order a meal for her mom.

When she left, Veronica pulled the duvet up to her chin and sobbed. Ashley had suffered enough with the recent death of her own husband. But to tell her the truth about her father was beyond cruel. Olivia also deserved the truth. She was going to hurt the people she loved most… with the truth.

"Maybe, just maybe, I should keep my mouth shut." She pursed her lips, angry at herself for years of weakness and deception. "The truth shall set you free. What a load of crap."

Her body twitched as she began to drift again into a troubled sleep.

The bell to the suite rang several times. She heard buzzing, and waved her hands, anxious.

"Mrs. Andersen?" Christopher glided across the wooden deck. When her eyes fluttered, he placed her lunch on the table next to her.

"Are you feeling okay, Ma'am?"

She stared at him, attempted to sit up then slumped back into the chaise lounge. "I'm fine. Thank you." Her voice was a whisper, raspy, congested. She waved him away.

Christopher smiled, bent toward her, a tray in his hand. Her shell-like hand reached up to his face.

"I like your dark hair, sir. Dark-haired men can be trusted."

He frowned. "Thank you, Mrs. Andersen." He strode away and left the suite. Once outside, he pulled out his cell and called Tony, hoping Olivia was with him.

"Tony, I think Olivia's mom needs help. Do you know where she is?"

"Yeah, right here with me. I'll let her know."

Tony hit the button on his phone. "Olivia, I think your mom needs you."

She shot him a look of pure frustration. "Come with me." A few minutes later they entered the deck area to find Veronica sitting upright, a bottle of wine in one hand, her other clenched around a smaller bottle.

Olivia gasped and covered her mouth.

Her mom mumbled something.

"What, Mom?"

"I'm sorry." She shifted in her chair. "I'm sorry." She dropped the plastic bottle.

Olivia stood rooted to the floor. She bent to retrieve the bottle, shaking it to find it empty. Then she saw the label. Ambien.

"Oh dear God, no. Mother?" She shook her mother's shoulder. "Mother, Mario is here. My father is here. Please!"

Her mom opened her eyes when she heard the name, Mario. She saw the panic on Olivia's face, glanced at the bottle in her daughter's hand and weakly laughed. "You silly girl. I threw those pills overboard. I wanted to take them, but before I die, I need to share a family secret." Her eyes closed, her breathing steady, and Veronica slept, her arms hanging limply by her side.

Tony watched the tears filling Olivia's eyes. He walked to her, wrapped her in his arms and let her cry.

"I want to hate her. But I can't," she mumbled between sobs.

He lifted her face to his and kissed her, wiping away her tears with his thumb.

Olivia breathed deeply, held his face between her hands and kissed him unleashing a passion she hadn't felt since her divorce. She pulled away, stunned, her heart drumming against her chest. This relaxing day at sea had turned sour too early in the day.

The lounge at the bow of the ship bounced to the beat of the evening's seventies music. People of all ages were crammed onto the dance floor doing the hand motions of the old YMCA song. Strobe lights waved over the masses while they gyrated, some unable to form the proper letters.

Others had difficulty with hand and feet coordination. Despite their clumsiness, they were completely uninhibited and having fun. The cruise director staff had attired themselves in ridiculous outfits and wigs, as everyone merged into one big party. I had to admit, it was quite the spectacle. Almost brought a smile to my face. Almost.

More than anything, I wanted to be on my private deck, quiet, alone, inhaling the salt air, great gulps of it, to cleanse my mind and body. But Mother was there, sitting by the pool, wrapped in her blankie and sulking. Ashley and Anders hovered, attempting to cheer her up and convince her to go to her room to watch a movie on television.

I'd left, feeling like I'd been stung by killer bees with the afternoon incident with the pills. Mother's cavalier attitude ticked me off. I almost wished she'd taken all the pills.

Her timing always perfect, she'd interrupted a special moment with Tony and ignored my panicked reference to Mario. I had no choice but to disappear into a crowd. I continued to push my way through the "young man" dancers to a far corner sheltered from the ricocheting lights and glitter. Except for a small candle in the middle of the two person table, the corner matched my dark mood. I leaned in to snuff the flame, realized it was electric, took the artificial object from its orange votive and turned off the battery. I slid into the red leather chair and, with my forehead against the cold window, looked down at the shimmering white froth as the ship plowed through the water.

I was definitely on a huge pity party. And, when the cocktail waitress approached me for a drink order, I waved her away, not caring if I was rude. I just wanted to be alone. And sometimes the best way to be alone is to disappear into a crowd of strangers.

Most of my life, I'd loved parties. Especially during my years married to Jon the jackass. Now, as I looked back, he'd been having the fun and I'd been watching. Always on the outside looking in. Who was I really? A product of an affair, a cold father who wasn't my father, missing out on a tender dad I'd just met, and never knowing my mother before her drinking days. I was mad at the world.

"Here's a quiet corner," bellowed a male voice.

I glanced to the side and inwardly groaned. The obnoxious man dressed in one of his many Hawaiian shirts, big, brash, and annoying…Dick Yoder. Not only could he fill a room, tonight he seemed to fill the whole dang ship. He had a gaggle of Red Hat Ladies with him. They giggled and squealed their way into the last few empty spaces on the perimeter of the lounge, following him like he was the Pied Piper. Now I was spitting mad and crunched my face into a scowl I was certain could become permanent.

"Hey, little lady, I'm buying drinks for everyone. What would you like?" He slapped me on the shoulder.

"Nothing, thank you," I said, turning away. *Little lady?*

And that's when I spied Tony. He strode to a section just below me but out of the glare of the lights, and sat in a chair next to blaring speakers. Odd. He never looked around the room. Just sat there, drink already in hand, head still, but I knew his eyes were moving. I'd noticed his ability to observe. It was disquieting. Even though I was behind him and several tables away, it was as though I was sitting next to a power line, my attraction to him was so strong. I turned so I could see him directly. But striding like a sleek panther was "Putin" guy from our dinner table, the quintessential bad boy from a Bond movie, thick with muscle, sexy and scary at the same time. He slid into a chair at the table next to Tony. He also had a drink in his hand.

I knew they were talking to each other. But they were speaking forward into space, not making eye contact. The hairs on my arm bristled.

"Hey, Carmella," yelled the flower- shirted guy. He waved his beefy hands. "Another round of drinks for the ladies here."

At that moment, Tony turned, our eyes met. He looked away.

I noticed a shrug of his shoulders. He stood, raised his glass to the Bond man, then walked towards me.

"Olivia. I thought you'd retired for the evening," said Tony, resting his hand on my shoulder. Power line back. Could anyone see the sparks?

"Carmella, sweetheart, drinks for this nice couple, too." Hawaiian shirt turned to Tony and extended his hand. "Seen ya around the ship, pal. I'm Dick Yoder. Pleased ta meet ya." His hand dwarfed Tony's.

"Hey, right back at you. I'm Tony. And this lovely lady is Olivia. We're at the same table for dinner."

Guess he wanted to make certain old Dick knew we had just met on the ship. Hmmm?

Dick had fished out a stack of business cards from his pants pocket and delivered them to all the Red Hats, me, Tony and even Carmella. "Here's my card. You ever need a Mercedes, I have the biggest dealership in Miami." He winked. "I'll give ya'll a deal you can't refuse," he whooped.

Carmella fumbled hers, and I noticed handwriting on the back of her card. Tony dropped his card and in a flash traded it with the one on Carmella's tray.

It seemed Tony was more than just a passenger. My body warmed. I sensed intrigue, danger, and intense excitement. Too much excitement.

"Tony, it's been a long day. And tomorrow I'm looking forward to seeing Taormina."

"You don't look tired, Olivia. Quite the opposite." He took my hand.

"Thanks for the compliment, Tony." I shrugged. "Always have to make sure my mom is taken care of and check on Ashley's plans." I glanced toward the group clustered around Mr. Yoder. "Besides, it's getting too loud in here."

"I'll walk you to you to the elevator," he said, placing his hand on my back.

I didn't want to leave him. "Good night, Tony." I leaned in to give him a kiss on the cheek. He stood watching me until the doors closed.

I had a date with Mario tomorrow in Taormina. But I couldn't shake the obvious intrigue of Tony. He excited me. He certainly seemed—clandestine? Two men in my life right now were a complete mystery. And I found myself ready for a wild ride!

Day Six – Port Of Messina, Sicily Gateway To Mount Aetna And The Ancient City Of Taormina

Olivia

Spidery clouds crawled across the gloomy gray sky as the ship eased into the Port of Messina. Mist sprayed from the hovering clouds. I wrapped my robe tighter and picked up the mug of hot coffee Christopher had poured for me. The steam curled upwards, blending into the overcast sky.

I loved waking early at a new port. Messina was quiet compared to the larger ports with their bustle of cargo containers and clamoring machinery. A six foot golden

Madonna smiled onto my deck as though blessing me. We passed so close to the *Madonna della Lettera,* set atop the Forte San Salvatore, I could almost touch her. Legend declared the city of ancient Messina received a letter from the Madonna saying she would always bless those coming in and out of the port. The daily paper from the cruise ship said the night lighting of this statue is actually controlled at the Vatican. I doubted the legend, but her smile seemed welcoming and kind. And it gave me extra hope for this particular day with my father, Mario.

My cell phone trembled on the side table, jiggling between the sugar and cream.

"Text Message" glowed on the screen. Mario never wasted words. "Meet me at Granduca Garden. 11:30. Corso Umberto #172. Everyone knows where it is. *Baci,* Mario."

I slipped the phone into my robe pocket and reached for a sweet roll. The roll stuck in my throat. I gulped some coffee. The truth was, between last night and this morning, my mind was spinning and my stomach churning about Tony, my mother and Mario. Today would be all about meeting Mario and a half sister. I needed to blot everything else from my mind. But I was engulfed with an uneasiness I could not shake.

The doorbell to my suite chimed loudly. I jumped and spilled my coffee. I put the coffee cup on the table and marched to the door. I knew my sister was on the other side…most likely with another problem. I grudgingly opened the door.

"Ashley. Good morning."

She walked past me and through my room to the balcony. "Don't you know you're not supposed to keep the balcony doors open? It causes humidity in the cabin."

"Thank you, dear sister. Is that what you needed to tell me so early this morning? Or perhaps there is something more urgent than an open door?" I bit my lip, too late to stem the dripping sarcasm. But words can't be unsaid. I shut the slider and invited her to sit on the deck chair.

"What's up, sis?"

"I don't know what to do with mom today and was wondering if you could take her for the day and give me a break?"

My stomach seethed. I was sure the coffee cream had just curdled in my already nervous stomach. I had to lie. No other way.

"Um, here's the thing, Ash. I've already arranged for a tour of Taormina with a few other people in a private van with a guide. There's no room for Mom, and it would be too strenuous for her anyway. But I can take her tomorrow in Malta." I leaned over to pat her arm, full of false sympathy.

She burst into tears. "I can't take it anymore. I have to get away from her."

At least I think that's what she said through her hands. Her shoulders heaved in time with her sobs.

"Ash, please. Stop crying. I can't understand you." I reached over to pull her hands away from her face and handed her a tissue from the coffee table. "Please, stop."

She turned luminous blue eyes towards me. "I just want her to die."

Whoa. I wasn't expecting *that.* "Ash, you and Mom have been so close. Why would you say that?"

"Because," she said, sobbing, "she won't stop talking about the past. She's saying horrible things about Dad and babbling about her 'lover' and destroying your life, and saying she's going to hell for what she did." She locked eyes with mine. "I need to get away from her."

"Wait. I'll call Christopher." I picked up the room phone and dialed his extension.

He answered on the first ring.

"Christopher, we need your help. This is Olivia. Can you arrange something for my mom today that would be easy and safe for her…just a couple of hours off ship with some nice people. Anything? And perhaps you could also arrange for someone to escort her back to her room for lunch and a nap?"

Christopher sighed. "Give me an hour to work on this. I'm sure the handicapped bus is going somewhere. She'll be well cared for, I promise."

I cradled the phone, looked at my sister and said, "Done. Now go and enjoy your day." I sighed with relief, and for the first time felt grateful for my sister's generosity on this cruise…especially for our butler, Christopher. He was magic. Give him a task and he completed it with a confident flair.

Ashley gave me her usual peck on the cheek, her tears blotted away, and with a wave of her hand, went to tell

Mother about the unexpected trip for her today. I listened at the door for a moment hoping for no protests. Hearing no yelling, I quietly shut the door and took a cleansing breath.

I put on a simple light blue sundress, a ruffled scarf, sandals, fixed my makeup and hair and disembarked. The long line of taxis snaked down the pier, eagerly awaiting fares. I grabbed the first one and said, "Taormina, please." The driver nodded, closed the door and began to weave through the city to the main road. He drove like Michael Andretti along the highway from the port to the city in the hills. Along the way, between frightening curves and breathtaking views, I thought about Tony.

He'd asked me to meet him for coffee this afternoon in Taormina. I'd been so nervous about running into him today I'd forgotten the name of the coffee shop. And I had no idea how much time Mario wanted to spend with me. I was certainly attracted to Tony. But my ex always sat on my shoulder reminding me of a failed relationship. And then all this secret agent stuff between Tony and blue-eyed beefy guy. I tried to remember his name. Joe sounded right.

My daydreaming was interrupted by the driver jolting to a halt and saying, "*Arriviamo.*"

"*Dritto e' Corso Umberto.*" The cab driver obviously spoke minimal English and had been mute on the drive to Taormina except for waving a hand at a passing tourist attraction. He pointed to a narrow street directly in front of me, smiled and held out his hand. I paid him sixty euro and stared in amazement. Taormina stood before me, a riotous blend of pink, gold, and beige buildings and curved wrought iron balconies. Red geraniums and purple wisteria dripped and drizzled over the iron and slid down the side of ancient stucco walls. Cars were not allowed inside the center of the town. But pedestrians flooded the narrow winding Corso Umberto snapping photos, shopping, and eating mouthwatering pastries.

I trembled at the thought of meeting my half-sister. Would she like me? Resent me? I walked down the street, gazing with wonder at the store windows. One shop's window held the famous marzipan candy shaped into fruit, the next store window was decorated with pottery of bright gold and yellows. The scent of cheese drifted out the door of a market where an aproned vendor beckoned me inside to sample one of the dozens of cheeses for sale. The designer shoe store had me longing for money to buy things I didn't need. Finally to my right stood a sidewalk sign reading "Granduco Gardens." Taking a deep breath, I pushed through the heavy glass door and walked into a jungle of vines surrounding the walkway, down a narrow stairwell, and into a dimly lit bar. Where was the dining room? A slim young man in black trousers, crisp white shirt, and black vest quietly folded white linen napkins.

"Scusa, dove il ristorante?"

"Dritto." He waved his arm toward a massive archway.

Once past the arch, sunlight flooded a patio infused with bright flowers. In the distance was Mount Etna, glowering at us with a hint of fire and copious amounts of smoke. The view from the patio showed not only the volcano but the deep aqua sea far below. I glanced around the patio and spotted Mario's glorious hair. Across the table from him sat a stunning woman, her raven hair cascading in rippling waves over her shoulders. Her dark eyes flashed in my direction and widened in disbelief. She could have been my twin, except for her continental beauty that was wild and natural and her dark chocolate eyes. Her eyes flashed in my direction and could have turned water into ice.

I paused.

Mario must have seen her gaze. He turned, and then stood, walking to me. His hands firmly grasped my shoulders as he kissed my cheeks. "Olivia. Come meet your sister, Mia."

I felt her assessment through the nod of introduction. Her expression remained serious and unsmiling. Was it dislike, shock, resentment? Mario held a chair for me and waited. I sat, feeling awkward and clumsy next to this natural beauty.

"Olivia," said Mario, taking my hand in his, "and Mia," he whispered, touching her chin, "I know this is awkward for both of you." Tears welled and leaked from his eyes. "But you must understand, this is a good thing."

Mia turned her full attention to her father. "I know, Papa', how difficult this has been for you." When she turned to me, I felt agitated. "You need to give all of us time," she said. "It's been quite difficult to understand," she paused, "this situation."

She swept her hair over her shoulders, her curls bouncing down her back.

"Olivia, please I ask you not to expect too much. I am still in shock." She looked away for a moment, and then she smiled. "There is no doubt we're sisters. However, do you have any idea what it's like to know my father was with another woman? In America? And had a child? My father has always been my hero. And this information has been stunning. You do understand, right?"

"Of course I understand. It's been a shock to me for most of my life," I answered.

There was complete silence.

Mia looked toward the sea, hands folded in her lap. After what seemed like an eternity, she turned to me and said, "It's frightening how much we look alike."

I laughed. "But you are prettier than I am, Mia. Much prettier."

Mario grinned. "Now everyone is happy, no?"

"No," said Mia. "Your sons are not happy, and are worried about Mama and their inheritance." She turned to me. "Olivia, you do know that sons are everything in Italy… and spoiled. Be prepared."

She looked back to her father. "Mama will be bitter. You betrayed her while you were engaged. I can't believe it." She rolled her deep brown eyes and grasped the menu in front of her. "I'm hungry. Maybe after some lunch and wine, we can talk." She perused the menu and turned to me. "Boys are everything in Italy," she repeated.

I looked out at the shimmering sea, took a deep breath, and picked up my menu. *Inheritance? What inheritance?* When I glanced toward the waiter, my stomach lurched. I thought I saw Ashley in the corner of the bar. When the woman turned her head to order, she was just another blonde. I breathed a sigh of relief. Ashley. I prayed she'd be on a mission to buy something from every store in port and would forget to eat, enjoy gelato, or people watch. If we ran into each other, I'd just have to lie, again.

"Olivia, look at the mountain." said Mario.

"Why?"

"Mount Etna is erupting. You need to watch it."

I turned and saw a vault of blue over billows of white smoke curling upward. It was magnificent.

"Papa'," said Mia. "Let's order our lunch."

"Please, you order for me," I said. "And then I want to know all about you."

"No. I think it's better that I know about you. How you found my papa', about your mother, your growing up in a home without a father." Her smile was cold. Her hard dark eyes narrowed, and there was no joy or sparkle. All the relief I'd just felt vanished along with my appetite. I returned her smile, but I felt sick.

"Ask me anything, Mia." I patted her arm and felt it stiffen. "Then I want to hear all about you."

I turned to Mario and rested my hand on his. "That's only fair, right, Mario?"

When I turned back to Mia, her lips were pursed and her brows furrowed. But I had dealt with Mother and Ashley all my life. Mia didn't stand a chance.

Although the food must have been incredible, at least it looked fabulous, I spent most of lunch pushing the bright red tomatoes and mozzarella cheese back and forth across my plate.

"Actually, Mia, I did not grow up without a father. I thought he was my dad until the day he died. My sister told me, one day, in a fit of anger, that I was adopted. It took a lot of searching over many years. But one day I found a locket. The photo inside was of a handsome dark-haired stranger who looked a lot like me. And I began to search in earnest."

I glanced at Mario, giving him a timid smile. "From that moment, I knew why I never fit into my blonde blue-eyed Nordic family."

I turned to Mia and looked directly into her eyes. "It's obvious we look like our *papa', si?*"

I made a mental note to take my language lessons more seriously.

She frowned in concentration, and with a show of reluctance, said, "It is obvious." Looking at Mario, she said, "Guess I don't know the whole story, Papa'." Once again she tossed her gleaming locks and shrugged. A gesture I knew I'd see a lot. "I think it's time you told me everything." Her voice was arctic cold.

Two hours later, with my rambling on researching family history, finding and contacting Mario, his explanation of how he felt learning of my existence, and other odds and ends, Mia started to soften…a bit. Her face relaxed, she intermittently patted her dad's arm, glanced at me with an occasional 'hmmm' as if she felt my pain, so to speak. And then she asked the question.

"Papa', are you sure mama doesn't know about this? Her temper has been worse lately."

"Not yet, Mia. Not yet." Mario leaned back and rubbed his jaw. "I wanted to meet Olivia first. I will tell Mama before the ship docks in *Venezia*." He closed his eyes, and then leaned forward.

With a heavy sigh, he took each of us by the hand and said, "Pray for me."

I stared at my hands, not knowing how to respond. I suddenly had a strange thought. Had I just been plunked into a culture run by women? It sounded like Mario was afraid of his wife.

The waiter slid the check for the lunch onto the table.

"Excuse me," said Mario. "I need to make a phone call and will pay for lunch. Be back in just a moment."

When Mario disappeared from the patio, Mia leaned in to me. "Let's get one thing straight. You are the intruder. You've turned our lives upside down. And you have no idea what your sudden appearance is going to do to my mother. Because of your mother, mine has never been properly loved by my Papa'. She's told me many times how things felt different after his year in America." She glared. "And now I know why."

I felt her anger humming all the way down to the soles of my sandals. "I didn't ask for this, Mia."

"Oh yes. You did. You had to find your birth father." Her words were whispered but emphatic. "You're dealing with another culture. Don't expect a big happy family welcome when you arrive in Venice…with your Mother."

"But…"

Mia held her hand up to stop me. "You might feel completed now. But you are going to find Italian families are very close. In a way, I pity you."

"Your father told me he loves your mother with all his heart. And that Veronica was just one of those romances of youth. Trust me, my mother is not a threat to anyone."

She glanced up to see Mario approaching and smiled. "Just remember what I've said." She patted my hand.

I knew, with searing clarity, it might take a lifetime for her to accept me. For the first time, the joy of finding my birth father faded into fear.

Mario returned, his smile as wide as a new day, unaware of the tension. "Ready, ladies?" Mario escorted us out of the restaurant, down the street to the taxi stand.

"I will text you soon, Olivia." His eyes welled as he kissed me goodbye.

Mia hesitated. "It will be good to see you in Venice, Olivia." She looked away, sighed, and turned back to me. "Family is family!"

She startled me with a hug and kissed me on both cheeks and whispered, "But remember what I said."

"Thank you, Mia. I think we all need time. But the joy I've found knowing my real father is impossible to describe. And I am happy to have found you." I leaned in and returned her hug to assure Mario all was okay, although I shivered inside from her coldness.

Mario paid the taxi driver and opened the door. He couldn't let go of my arm. *"Ti volgio bene, Olivia."*

I leaned back into the soft leather seat and closed my eyes. I mulled over the stories shared at lunch, dozed for a bit, and jumped when the driver opened my door.

"Arriviamo, Signora. Arriviamo."

I reached into my purse and gathered twenty euro from the zippered lining for a tip.

"Grazie, Signora."

I groggily boarded the ship, went directly to my suite, wrote a note to my sister and mom telling them not to disturb me, assured Ashley I would take Mom to Malta the next day, entered my room and locked the door.

I flopped on the bed and fell asleep at once. My cell phone woke me up. Glancing at my watch, I saw it was nine. I'd missed dinner and Tony.

"Olivia, are you okay?"

"Tony, it's been a rough day."

"Want to meet for a drink in the lounge? No party there tonight."

"I'm sorry, but I'm going to stay in tonight. I'll see you tomorrow at dinner. I promised Ashley I'd take Mom for the day in Malta."

"Okay. But something in your voice. I'm concerned."

Just hearing his voice gave me chills…the good kind.

"Well, if it will ease your concerns about me, how about we meet in the strings lounge where it's dark and quiet. Give me an hour. But I have to warn you, I'm a disheveled mess."

I heard a sigh. "Thank you, Babe. I need you tonight."

I closed the phone and ran to the shower. He needed me. I needed him. We'd be safe in the lounge. No going to each other's rooms. Just being together would be enough for now.

I trembled, looking for Tony, nervous and excited. He was near a window in a dimly lit corner. Music played from the speakers. I walked slowly toward him. He stood, waiting.

"You're beautiful, Olivia." He pulled me to him and enveloped me into his arms. We held each other for several delicious moments before he guided me to my seat.

He offered me a glass of wine. "A toast to us." His dark eyes mesmerized me.

Our glasses touched, we took a slow sip, and he pulled me next to him, not speaking for a long time.

Day Seven – Port Of Valletta, Malta

Olivia

*M*y one hour with Tony in the lounge listening to the string quartet last night had been magical. He'd held my hand, nuzzled my neck with kisses, and murmured over and over…when we get to Venice, Olivia…and his voice would drift. I'd hoped he'd ached for me as I did for him. I had grudgingly left for my room to get much needed sleep. But my mind was scrambled with images of Mario, Mia, my mother, and Tony.

So I found myself on the balcony, cuddled in my robe, at six a.m. watching a beige city. Once we entered the protected harbor of Valletta, it felt like modern civilization has disappeared. Limestone battlements and an ancient fort jutted into the sea, massive baroque cathedrals, church towers, and arched doorways lined the steep hillside and popped clearly into view. But they seemed terribly out of place and a bit foreboding.

On closer look, Valletta Harbor appeared less beige and more cream-colored, with climbing buildings and twisting streets, hillsides…all pockmarked from centuries of cannon fire, almost as though someone had carved it from the sand of the sea.

Centuries-old ancient forts guarded the harbor entrance. And colorful little luzzo boats…a fishing craft resembling an elf's shoe, bobbled in the early morning light. I'd read in the ship paper about Michelangelo designing the port of Valletta. The port was lovely, and I started to feel excited about exploring this historic island until I remembered I had Mom for the day.

I reached for the room phone on the wall and called Christopher. I ordered an entire pot of coffee.

Veronica knocked on my door at nine. "I'm ready, dear. Oh my, you look so tired. Are you okay?"

"I'm fine, Mom. Just fine. Take a seat on the deck. I'll be a few more minutes."

I dressed in white capris and a bright peacock-blue jersey top. Grabbed a visor. It was going to be hot today, and there was little shade in the old part of town.

Mother held my arm as we disembarked, and I spotted Christopher right away. He walked us to our taxi, and handed me an umbrella to protect my mom from the heat.

"Thanks, Christopher," I said. "You seem to think of everything."

By mid-morning, the heat was formidable. I knew my mother would wilt if I didn't get her inside. Heck, I was melting. The walled city of Valletta was an intricate monochromatic beige in richly varied shades, full of life, and it glowed as though a living stone. I found myself feeling immense regret I couldn't explore this unique island by myself. But a promise was a promise. Ashley had the day to herself, and I had Mom.

Christopher had ordered the driver to take us to a charming café in the middle of the main street. Caffe' Cordina lived up to my expectations…clean, air-conditioned, elegant…and good food. Since we planned to tour the city later by a horse and buggy, I'd thought it best to start with a snack and have a late lunch before returning to the ship. Mother seemed in good spirits today, hadn't whined about anything yet. She seemed to be tolerating the heat and hadn't complained at all. Between the umbrella and the air-conditioning, she kept cool. But it was early.

We sat inside by the window overlooking the outdoor patio. I ordered café lattes and cream horns. In the shape of a horn, the puff pastry is filled with jam or whipped cream. The outside was crispy, coated with sugar. It was the special pastry of Malta. The display case held so many different mouthwatering treats, and I couldn't wait to munch on one. The water bottle in the center of the table was deep blue and cold. I poured the water into our crystal glasses and paused, assessing mom. The waiter returned with our coffees.

Her usually bright blue eyes were red-rimmed and watery, her thinning hair buried under a large gaudy hat. Her clothes hung loosely on her body accentuating her drastic loss of weight in recent months. I had a rush of sympathy and love for her.

Mom sat and stared out the window with empty eyes, her coffee cold and untouched. She seemed far away, distant, insulated and wrapped in the numbness of alcohol as she had been throughout my childhood. The memory felt like a deep bruise. She turned to me, this time eyes brimming with tears, and rested her hand on mine.

"Olivia, we need to talk."

"Mom, please. Not now. Can't we just enjoy the day? Really?"

She forged ahead. "I must tell you about your real father." She whispered the word 'father' as though it were sacred. "Your father was or rather is an incredible man. I honestly don't know if he's dead or alive. I only wish I'd spent the last thirty-five years with him."

"Mother, please. I know Daddy adopted me." I felt my body tense as though I were in a vise. "And it didn't take a brain surgeon to figure out I wasn't a part of the alabaster-skinned, blond-haired, blue-eyed family in which I was raised. Give me some credit." I rolled my eyes and withdrew my hand, clasping them together in the folds of the dark green cloth napkin on my lap.

"It was also obvious you and Eric were not happy. Nor were you happy after he died. I understand those things. What I don't understand is why you turned to alcohol and stayed with it after he was gone."

"I want to tell you about it. I'm dying, Olivia." Her gaze held mine for a moment. Then her eyes cast downward. "Nothing matters to me but you. I don't need your forgiveness." She covered her mouth and coughed. It sounded like sandpaper on rough wood. "I just want you to know everything. You deserve nothing less."

"It's okay, Mom. You're not feeling well, and, I know all I need to know for now." I took her hand in mine. "I'm fine." I lowered my voice, patted her hand and entwined my fingers, trying to calm myself. She did need my forgiveness. But most of all, I needed to forgive her.

The sharpness of my tone and words wiped any shine out of her eyes. But it didn't stop her.

"Your father's name is Mario. It's strange. I've been dreaming about him lately. I even thought you said his name to me." She glanced back to the window and sat quietly, her mind wandering far from Malta. When she turned her gaze to me, it was thoughtful.

"You know, Olivia, I've always loved you best. You were born out of love."

My jaw dropped. Ashley had been the favorite. Always. And love didn't keep secrets about real fathers.

"I see you don't believe me." She tried to chuckle, causing another wracking cough. "Ashley didn't need me. She had her father, who doted on her like she was royalty. He loved you, too. But…in reality, his first-born Ashley was his princess." Her hands rested on the edge of the table. She looked at them almost as though they belonged to someone else.

"Even before you knew the truth about Eric, you always struggled to feel part of the family. You thought I didn't notice. I remember feeling physically ill sometimes watching you." She glanced up to me, then looked back down.

When she looked at me again, her features had contorted into anger. "I hated Eric. That's why I drank. It was weak and shameful. By the time I was thirty, I had hard lines on my face. He promised me the world, and then cheated on me. I could never please him." A strange icy expression moved across her face.

"Before Mario left, we agreed to never see each other or make contact. To protect Ashley." A grim smile twisted her face. "I didn't realize I was pregnant. And, God only knows, I was too stupid to think you might look like him…with his dark skin and gray eyes. You have his smile, you know." Her lips parted and a slow unspeakable sadness crept into her eyes.

A sudden seething anger flared inside me. But I shook it down deep inside where the rest of my anger and pain was hidden. I couldn't deal with her problems anymore. I didn't want to know the truth of what she'd suffered. I only wanted to be with my real father and move on. But she looked so pitiful, this woman who had birthed me. So fragile and unhappy.

The waiter slid our plates covered with cream horns toward us, looked at us for a moment, then bowed and slipped away.

I glared at her. "Why didn't you leave Daddy? Why?"

I felt guilty for asking this question of my mother only because she was dying. I'd often wondered why he didn't leave her, this woman who drank.

"What could I have done? Where would I have gone? I had no skills to get a job and take care of a child. Eric was wealthy, and he made a comfortable life for me. Only it was a miserable life." She sighed.

"I don't want to talk about this. I only want time with you, Mother. Today. Let's just enjoy Malta."

"That's always your way, Olivia. Avoidance. You get that from me. Don't think about it and the problem will disappear." Her voice rose. "Well, you're not going to avoid this."

"Oh, yes, I am." I grabbed a horn and bit into it, the cream oozing onto my fingers. I took a sip of my latte followed by a gulp of cold water. "I know as much as I want to know. You did the best you could as a mom. I did the best I could as a wife. Somewhere along the way, we both were too weak to do the right thing."

Mom's lips pursed into a pout. "Nobody prepares us for marriage or motherhood. I just didn't do right by you."

I touched her hand, sighed, and looked away.

I caught a glimpse of people from our ship ambling by enjoying the beauty of the city, looking normal and happy. That's when the dam broke and the rage I'd felt all my years burst. The unfairness of my childhood, living with an alcoholic mom who was like having no mom at all, discovering my adoption, finding my birth father. A scream rose in my throat, threatening to erupt like lava from Mt. Etna. But I stopped it, breathed deeply and managed once again to gain a semblance of control, shoving the rage down deep where I'd kept it for so long. I banged the delicate glass of water on the table. It shattered, splashing cold water onto my lap.

I was happy for the spill. I needed a distraction. Blotting my wet clothes with the napkin, I struggled to compose myself. But I was fuming, feeling like a child, unhappy, not understanding anything about my family.

Through gritted teeth, I said, "Now we're going to catch our buggy tour of Valletta. And we're going to enjoy the ancient walled city with its convoluted history and beautiful architecture." I stood up, fished some money from my purse, flung it on the table, and stood behind my mother's chair.

I apologized to the waiter for the mess I'd made.

"Get up, Mom." She looked at me with a sigh. She didn't move.

"Please, Mom. We can talk about this in the privacy of our suite."

She sighed again, but pushed back her chair, defeated as she always had been. Except there was no alcohol waiting for her in a hidden closet. Just a day in the fresh air with her dark-haired daughter.

Relief flooded through me. The tour and Malta would be the escape I needed. I tucked my mom's arm into mine and gently guided her out the door.

Turning to my left, I spotted the horse and buggy. A smiling guide perched on the seat behind the horse.

"Look, Mother. There's our ride."

She turned and made a face. "Horses smell so bad… and in this heat."

Relieved to find my normal complaining Mother back to her old self, I relaxed.

"My name is Umberto," the guide said as he jumped from the buggy. His attire was worn but clean and neat, starched white shirt tucked into black trousers, a black fedora on his head. His smile was as wide as the Island of Malta and it reassured me I could have a pleasant day, despite how I felt about my dysfunctional mother.

He gently guided my mom into the carriage, helped me up, and started non-stop talking about his beloved Malta.

The mid-morning sun was unrelenting in the tree-free city of Valletta. Our driver offered us umbrellas and deferred to my mother's weak state and obvious bad health with lively chatter and gentle interaction with her.

"Again, my name is Umberto. I was born on this beau-tiful island of Malta. How are you lovely ladies today?"

"I'm Olivia and this is my mother, Veronica."

He smiled. "But you are too young to have a daughter," he said, winking at my mom.

She returned his smile, sitting up straight, and said, "Thank you. You're very kind."

"I'll tell you about the places we will visit," he said, his voice was soft. It was if he knew Veronica was very ill, and he wanted to show her great respect.

I took her hand in mine and enjoyed the tour, frequently daydreaming, listening to the clip clop of the horses hooves. Forgiveness would come. I knew now, with certainty, forgiveness was the only road I could take. To heal myself, I would have to forgive my mother. I loved my Mom, and I needed to show my love. But how do you show love to someone who's unable to return it?

Mario

He shivered, pulling his jacket close to him despite the sunflower-bright day, pleasantly warm for Venice at this time of year.

The chill came from his daughter's coldness. His son-in-law, Eduardo, and Mia had driven him from the airport to the Number One water bus. She'd not spoken in the car.

"Thanks for the ride," he said, throwing as much warmth into his voice as possible.

"My pleasure," said the beaming Eduardo.

Mia nodded, no smile.

"Remember," Mario said. "I'm telling your mother tomorrow at the penthouse." He waited for a response.

"We'll be there, Papa'," said Mia. "You know Mama. There'll be a lot of drama. You have no idea how badly Mother will respond to this."

Mario shrugged and turned toward the ticket booth, bought his ticket, trudged to the *Linea* 1 sign and waited.

What will I say to my Angela? He zipped his jacket and draped a brick red scarf around his neck.

He shuffled onto the waterbus, searching for a seat in a quiet corner, a rare commodity in crowded Venice, sat down and stared at the dark water of the Grand Canal. He pictured Olivia, kind, lighthearted, so much like him. Had she researched everything about him, his wealth, his business? Mia had planted doubt in his mind. But he owed Olivia something more than love.

The villa appeared, majestic and colorful. He waited with dread for the next stop, just before the Piazza San Marcos. He crossed himself and said a silent prayer.

Ten minutes later, he walked into the grand foyer of his city home. He missed his villa in the country. Never had felt right in the city. But this was Angela's place of birth, and he kept the property to mollify her.

He looked up the narrow staircase and plodded his way up…one, two, thirty-five, seventy. He reached for his key, opened the door and was greeted by the aromas of risotto and seafood. Angela had cooked a welcome-home meal.

"Mario, is that you?" Her voice was sweet and clear.

"It's me," he answered, taking off his jacket and hanging it neatly on the hall tree.

Angela came out of the kitchen, her plump frame bouncing with happiness.

"You're in a good mood," he said, drawing her close. "Let me hold you a minute. Hmmmm. You smell like a cross between the sea and a garden of roses."

She reached up and kissed him full on the mouth. Her green eyes glowed, makeup applied to perfection, her long, out-of-control blond curls tamed by a headband. She was still a beauty at sixty.

"I'm happy because all my boys are here for dinner." She wiped a loose tendril behind her ear. "Even Mia is coming."

"Why are the boys here? I wanted time alone with you." He smiled, pulling her back into an embrace, his chin resting on the top of her head. He breathed in Angela's scent, dreading the evening. He sighed. Now the kids would be here, adding to the drama.

She pulled back. "What's wrong? You seem tense." And as quickly as she'd beamed a smile, her face contorted into worry.

"Nothing's wrong, *caramia*. Let me wash up from the trip." He kissed her neck and walked toward the washroom, his heart pounding. Over the flow of running water, he heard the front door slam, followed by his boys howling for their mama. Luca and Adriano adored her.

"Smells fantastic," said Luca, his voice echoing from one plastered yellow wall to the other.

He heard Angela squeal with delight. He knew Luca had lifted her off the floor and twirled her around the kitchen.

Angela spoiled those boys. Still prepared meals, washed and ironed for them, cleaned up after them. It irritated him to no end. They were men, thirty and thirty-two. They needed to find wives and have babies. Mario shook his head in disgust and walked slowly into the kitchen.

Luca was fair like his mother, slender but muscular and quite impish. He hugged Mario with enthusiasm, kissing him on both cheeks.

Adriano was dark like himself, handsome with an undeniable natural sensuality. His dark curly hair and arresting green eyes made women swoon. He was spoiled and indulged by the female population and had an ego the size of Europe. He gave Mario a crushing hug.

Dinner was cheerful enough, but Mario felt the underlying tension with his sons. They knew about Olivia. No details. But according to Mia, they were not happy about an interloper in the family, let alone how hurt their Mama would be. They cared nothing about the pain Olivia had suffered.

"So how was your trip to Sicily, Papa'?" Adriano's voice dripped with sarcasm. "Sell a lot of wine?"

"Your sister's the salesperson in this family. She sold some of our reserve Chianti to a new German restaurant in Taormina. That girl could sell the skin back to a snake."

"I'm a snake, Papa'?" Mia and Eduardo slid quietly to the table. She'd changed into jeans and sweatshirt, her hair wild and loose.

"Go, everyone," said Angela. "I'll bring the food to the table." Dinner was uneventful with lots of small talk. Angela seemed unaware of tension. But Mario knew it would soon change. He listened to the chatter and tried to enter the conversation. But his head and heart were filled with doubt, dread, anger. He knew keeping this information about Olivia was a mistake, and it screamed wrong. He'd never forgotten Veronica and certainly had been unaware of a child. He should have told Angela the moment he knew about his daughter in California. For the last thirty-six years he'd thought and relived his time in Los Angeles. The consequences of youth sometimes reached far into the future. In his case, thirty-six years and a continent. But from the day Olivia "found" him, everything changed. The load of guilt had crushed him, distracted him and kept him up at night.

The emails and photos and now the precious times looking into his daughter's eyes had given him courage. How could he deny her his love? His eyes began to fill. He stretched and rubbed his eyes in feigned tiredness.

"Go to the living room, everyone. I'm going to make the espresso." Angela scurried to the kitchen, blissfully happy to be waiting on her family.

"So are you all going home now?" asked Mario.

Luca looked coldly at him. "We're not going anywhere until you talk to her and tell her everything."

"Tell me what?" asked Angela, balancing six cups on a silver tray. She'd removed her apron and looked lovely in her beige slacks and cream sweater. Although plump, she still had delightful curves in the right places. And Mario loved every inch of her.

Mario gazed at her face, so young looking. He patted the cushion and Angela cuddled up next to him.

"So. What must you tell me?" She glanced at the boys and her daughter and stiffened at their expressions.

Mario inhaled deeply. "There's no easy way, Angela. I wanted to tell you alone, but the kids wouldn't allow that. So I'm just going to state the facts and fill in details later. But first I want to tell you I'm so sorry."

Her eyes clouded, the green deepening into that stormy look he always feared. He took her hand.

"Remember that year, right after our engagement when I worked for the Italian Embassy in Los Angeles at my father's request? He wanted me to work on the import and export business, become familiar with the laws?"

"I remember," she said, methodically drawing out the syllables, almost asking a question.

"I was lonely."

Mario watched her movement, saw the rigidity, anger simmering just beneath the surface. She pursed her lips and turned to face him. "Go on…" She clasped her hands together.

"I met a woman, had a brief affair, and a child was conceived." He raked his fingers through his hair. "Now let me explain."

He heard Angela catch her breath. He was afraid to look at her. "I never knew about the child, but she found me. I met her on the Isle of Capri last week. Mia met her in Taormina while we were on our business trip."

He turned to face Angela. "It meant nothing. I came home, married you and we've had a wonderful life."

Angela scowled.

"I'd like the family to meet her."

Angela slapped Mario's face with a fury that stunned him.

"*Porco misurio, bastardo, imbecile.*" She picked up a book on the end table and threw it across the room. "Get out! Now!"

"Angela, it was 35 years ago."

Luca held her arms. She tried to twist away. "Stop, Mama, please listen," he said, restraining her.

"You haven't heard the whole story," Mario pleaded.

Angela picked up a vase, her face red with anger. "She wants money, doesn't she? "

Now Adriano was on his feet.

"No! No! She just wanted to know her real father," Mario pleaded.

Mia smiled, but it was a cold smile. "*We're* your family."

Mario put his face in his hands. "I can see I should have kept this quiet."

"Who the hell is the mother of this girl?" Angela narrowed her eyes. "Tell me."

"Olivia's mother is dying of cancer. She's an alcoholic and has no idea Olivia has contacted me." He splayed his hands. "My daughter needs a family."

Angela dropped the blue Murano vase and watched it shatter across the floor. Mia ran to her, hugging her.

With the rage Mario had dreaded, Angela looked directly at him, eyes narrowed, hands trembling, and said, "*fuori subito!*" She slammed her fist into the V of her left arm, turned, walked into the bedroom and slammed the door.

Mario stood like a statue. He knew she'd be angry. Yet he was stunned.

Tony

Tony pushed his way through the somewhat bedraggled-looking tourists wandering around the main square of Valletta. The clouds had finally retreated and he looked out on the twinkle of the Aegean Sea.

Tony spotted the loud tourist in the flowered shirt, Yoder, as he called himself. He was with Carmella, the flamboyant waitress from the ship. By now, he knew Yoder was a Russian, and he'd grown weary of his loud mouth and reptilian smile. He tailed them, but the hordes of ship people, always gathered in groups of thirty or forty, impeded his ability to observe. He was desperate to see if they were meeting someone on the island. His assumption about Carmella…she was just an opportunist looking to make some cash on the side.

They ducked down an alley toward the seaside. It appeared they were either meeting someone, trying to find a taxi, or both. He sidled alongside the storefronts to avoid the crowds and turned right at the alley. It was narrow, empty except for the Russian and the waitress. Tony had to pull back. He ambled, almost tiptoeing to avoid them hearing his footsteps. The cobblestones and giant walls, empty of windows or doors, made every sound bounce off the walls like cannon blasts.

They turned left at the end. The sea peeked with glitter at the end of the alley, a slice of sun cutting like an arrow along the walls. Tony pounded over the stones to catch up with them just as they piled into a taxi.

He took the next one in line. "Follow that taxi, please. Do you understand?"

"Yes, sir."

"I'll pay you double the fare if you don't lose them." Tony wiped his brow, moist with sweat from heat and anxiety.

"No problem. I need the money." The cab driver smiled, showing a row of gold teeth, and gripped the steering wheel hard, staring toward his target.

Twenty minutes later, they entered the tony town of St. Julian's, north of Valletta. Tony handed the driver a wad of euros and started to follow, catching a glimpse of the flowered shirt on the promenade along the bay.

They stopped to admire a statue of a boy holding a fish, ready to throw it to the nearby bronzed cat. And that's when the action began.

Two Chinese men approached them, and from the park near the statue about ten Filipino workers from the ship joined Yoder and Carmella. Tony leaned against the rail and held his phone steady, taking shot after shot.

He dialed his boss.

"What's happening?" his handler asked.

"You were right. It's a damn scheme to hire crew to abandon ship and work for the mob, probably in the sweat shops for the fashion industry. I've double checked. And this dude, Josef, is mean and reports to the Camorra. Don't see any Camorra on site, though. What should I do? I'm uploading photos to you now. "

"Got 'em. Get back to the ship. Meet me in your cabin at five. And Tony, stay invisible."

"One more thing," said Tony. "Christopher may be a double. I see him sipping a coffee as we speak, about twenty feet from the statue, watching."

"Get out of there now. Christopher is not a problem."

He paused. "And, Tony, we have two issues. I'll fill you in later. Guarantee it'll be resolved before the end of the cruise."

With a click, the phone went dead. Tony backed up and away from the bar where Christopher sat on the far side of the group of men and the lone woman, Carmella. He turned into the nearest store and was greeted by a woman's voice.

"Tony, what are you doing in St. Julian's? Isn't it the most charming little seaside town?"

He turned and looked directly into the bright blue eyes of Ashley. "Hey," he said, trying to think of an excuse for his presence.

"I'm buying gifts for my family and friends," said Ashley. "This jewelry store is just exquisite. Come see what I'm thinking of buying for Olivia. I'm hoping she likes it. You shopping for anything particular?"

"Nope. The heat is unbearable today, and I slipped in here for some air-conditioning. Feels good to avoid the heat, right? I also wanted to avoid crowds, so took a taxi here. Had read about St. Julian's on the internet before I boarded ship."

And while Tony walked to the jewelry counter laden with more sparkles than the sea outside, he came up with a plan. A cover, so to speak.

"Say, Ashley, I'm on my way back to the ship. Want to share a cab with me?"

"Sure, Tony. I need to check out a shoe store down the street and then I'll be ready. It felt so good to have a day to myself, not worrying about my mother or anyone for that matter."

Tony rested his hand on her arm. "I understand completely. Sometimes being alone is a great thing. And I know being a caretaker for your Mom has been tough. I hope you enjoyed your quiet day, but now I'm ready for some company. Care to indulge me?"

She gave him a sly smile. "Too bad Olivia isn't here. She'd be glad to keep you company."

"Well, I'm sure I'll see her at dinner tonight," he said.

He watched as she gathered the attractively wrapped presents and paid the bill.

"Want a drink?" Ashley asked, putting her arm through Tony's.

"Wouldn't mind, but could we wait until we get back to Valletta and nearer to the ship? I know a great café where they have fabulous pastries, right in the town center."

Tony escorted her, sure onlookers would assume they were together and entered the over-priced shoe store with her. Twenty minutes later, and four pairs of shoes in bulky boxes he gallantly offered to carry, they grabbed a taxi and went for the drink.

With any luck, the flower-shirted guy would pass right by them while they were sitting in the café. Even Christopher might stroll by. Tony felt a small amount of relief his cover hadn't been broken yet.

Venice. His goal in Venice would stun a lot of people. But he was done with the lonely undercover work, being "handled," lying. He couldn't do it anymore. He hated looking over his shoulder, wondering if his life would end, yearned for normal…something he'd never experienced in his adult life. He thought about Olivia. And his friend's vineyard in Northern California. He cringed at the thought of giving up his enormous salary. But money sure wasn't buying him happiness now.

"Tony?" Ashley nudged him. "Are you getting out with me? We're at the café." Her puzzled look confirmed his decision. Normal.

"Hey, sorry. I was daydreaming." He jumped out of the taxi, offering a hand for her, and then retrieved her packages. He felt, for a nanosecond, lightness in his feet.

The Café Caravaggio was crammed with ship people having their last drink of the day before boarding. The bright magenta umbrellas provided welcome shade from the searing afternoon sun.

"I hear this place is known for their white Caravaggio wine and pizza *Quattro Stagione*. Actually Christopher, our butler, recommended the place. He should know since he's been at this port for the last five sailings. Up for it?"

"Anything is fine with me," said Ashley as she stacked her packages under the table.

Tony's eyes roamed the tables for familiar faces. As soon as the wine arrived, Mr. Yoder wandered by, alone. Quiet, as though he didn't have a care in the world.

Tony smiled. "Ashley, thank you for a nice break. Let's toast to a great time at sea tomorrow."

Tony glanced at the architecture of the famous St. John's Cathedral next to them. He took a bite of the pizza, juice dripping down his chin and leaned in to chat with Ashley. Normal. I'm starting to feel normal. He'd found her annoying most of the time because of the tension between her and Olivia. But this afternoon, he'd discovered her charm and her intelligence. She knew a lot about art and talked incessantly about the treasures in Malta. He'd settled back into a calm and enjoyable state of mind, forgetting everything about his job.

Day Eight
Mediterranean Sea
Cruising DaY

From my balcony, the sea surface sparkled like ten-thousand diamonds. Soft feathers of sea air danced around me filling my lungs with purity, the salty spray sticking to my skin. I loved its tingle. Paradise. Alone, sipping my fresh coffee, nothing to see but water…wanting to stay here all day.

But Mario's text this morning had jolted me.

Cara Olivia, Tell about me today. Be her friend. Famiglia. Baci, Mario.

I knew he was right. The sick feeling in my stomach told me how difficult this was going to be for all of us.

With a sigh, I got up and walked over the soft blue carpet to the generic white phone in my room, dialed Ashley's number, and waited.

"Hullo." Her gravelly voice made it obvious I'd awakened her.

"Hi, Ash. Sorry about the early call. But I need to talk to you, without Mom around. It's important." I felt the pitch of my voice rising.

"Sure, Olivia." She yawned and sighed. "What time and where?"

"It's eight-thirty now. Just come to my balcony. Won't take long," I lied. "I have croissants and coffee."

"Fine. Be there in a few."

I opened the door to my suite, jammed a shoe beneath it to hold it open, and padded back to the balcony. The gauzy curtains fluttered delicately in the breeze. I arranged the chairs on either side of the round white table, making it easier to eat and talk. I sat down and waited.

An hour later, Ashley appeared, fully made up, wearing a bright yellow caftan. The contrast between the two of us was so startling it made me smile. I turned my tussled bed hair and mascara-caked eyes to her and laughed.

"My dear sister. You always look perfect. Sit."

I poured her fresh coffee.

"Now, Olivia. What's all the drama? I mean, you sounded like this was a serious conversation. I have a lunch date with Anders."

I held my hand up. "Stop. There might not be anything with Anders today because we're going to hash something out now. It might take minutes or hours. But the conversation will end when I am satisfied with the answer."

"You've always been such a pushover, Olivia. Where'd the courage come from? And don't talk down to me." She sipped her coffee, looking over the rim of the cup with those enormous blue eyes, blinking rapidly, set the cup down, and got up. She walked to the balcony rail and pulled out a shimmery sterling-silver cigarette holder from the pocket of her caftan.

"And when did you start smoking again, Ash?"

Still facing the sea, she said, "After Miles died. And don't judge me. Between losing my husband and dealing with our mother, I'm lucky it wasn't prescription drugs," she paused. "Or worse."

She shook out a Virginia Slim, holding it between her lips while fetching a lighter from her other pocket. The lighter flared and Ashley's meticulously manicured fingers touched it to the end of the cigarette. She inhaled deeply, blowing the smoke upward into the formerly clear air. She returned to her chair, took a sip of coffee and used the delicate blue bone china saucer as an ash tray.

"So," she said. "What do you want from me, Olivia?"

"There's no other way to say it. I've met my birth father."

"Here?" Her eyes widened. "You're kidding, right?"

I paused. "Yes. Here in Italy." I breathed deeply, waving away the fumes from her cigarette.

"While on this cruise?" Ashley's eyes ratcheted wider. She banged her cup onto the table. "What the hell are you trying to pull, Olivia? This cruise was for the three of us. To make her last days together with her family. Just you and me and our mom."

"What the HELL does that have to do with anything? Did you hear what I just said? I found my birth father. Please respond to that *fact*, Ash."

She sat quietly for a few moments, her body starting to sag, as though someone had deflated her.

"Your father? Our father is dead."

"Are you hard of hearing? I said my BIRTH father. You know. The man mom had an affair with all those many years ago. Like thirty-five years ago, to be precise. Oh wait. That's when I was born. Okay. Thirty-six years ago."

"I thought you'd put that behind you." Tears formed in the corners of her eyes. She looked apprehensive.

The silence felt loaded. She averted her eyes, pulling smoke in, exhaling slowly. I said nothing. Just watched her. Everything about her smelled of money and a glamour glossy magazine model. But inside, I knew she hurt. I could almost see an invisible wall being put up, brick by brick. The only thing missing was an alligator-filled moat and a drawbridge. Ashley had been building a fortress around herself for a long time, ever since she left home. Fortress Ashley. But I couldn't stay silent.

"Put it behind me? You told me when I was twelve years old I was adopted in the back yard of our home.

You were my older sister, home for the summer. Mother brushed it off like it was no big deal. And, with sudden clarity, I saw how much I didn't fit into this corn-flower blue-eyed family, and why my dark hair, skin, and smoky gray eyes weren't a fluke of nature, but a blending of genes."

"Stop shouting. You'll wake Mother up. She'll be upset."

"I don't care anymore. Because, dear half-sister, MOTHER is going to meet Mario in Venice. And you are going to help me prepare her for this meeting."

"Are you insane? You can't do that to her. Have you forgotten she's dying?"

"I'm well aware she's dying. Right now, at this moment, it isn't about Mom. This is about me! Can you give me this, Ashley? I need to know the truth." I snatched a croissant, and bit angrily into it, biting my tongue as well. My hands balled into fists, the nails gouging into my palms. "Did you honestly think I would bury that revelation and not do something about it?"

Ashley squared her shoulders, took a deliberate breath, and reached over to push some hair from my forehead. "You were like a baby doll to me. From the day you were born, you were mine. I didn't learn the truth until I was older. But it made no difference to me."

My mind throbbed with memories crashing into one another. Ashley holding me, feeding me, dragging me along with her friends. Ashley screaming at me, calling me a brat, accusing me of making Mom unhappy. Some images still felt like open wounds.

"What happened, Ash? I need to know. How did you find out? And put out the disgusting cigarette. The smoke is making me choke."

She turned her head away and looked blank, smashed the ashes into the saucer, looked down, wringing her hands, and whispered, "I heard Dad hitting Mom. It was awful."

The quiet echoed like a ticking clock, awkward silence shadowed by a deep sadness.

Ash wrapped her arms around her shoulders. "Daddy started to say mean things about Mom." She covered her face with her hands and started to sob. She dabbed her face with a napkin and gazed into my eyes. "He tried to blame all of his misery on her."

"Sounds like him."

Another long pregnant silence.

"And one more thing," I said. "After Dad died, Mom started to wear a locket."

"I remember."

"I looked inside it and understood."

I hugged myself tightly, bracing for the words.

"What did you understand?" She looked at me.

"I understood who I was, who I looked like, why I felt like an outsider in our family. Why Dad ignored me and favored you. And I figured I was the reason Mom turned to alcohol."

My stomach twisted in knots, and I waited for Ashley to respond.

The silence roared like an explosion. Ashley clenched her fists, her expression full of misery. "Dammit!" She reached for a glass of water, clutching the slender stem so tightly I thought she'd break it.

"Please, Ash. What is it?" I wasn't feeling especially magnanimous, but I wanted her to reveal everything.

"Olivia, you've always said you felt like you were on the outside looking in…the odd person with the dark hair and skin…" Her voice quivered. "It was me on the outside."

"What?" It was my turn to stand up and hit the railing. I leaned on it, angry. I heard a happy family playing shuffleboard on the deck below, yelling in joy when the disc landed on a point. I couldn't remember a time when my family had laughed together.

"Explain to me, Ash, how you were the outsider. Are you looking at me clearly? You look exactly like Mother, with Dad's angular jaw and his long frame. There is NOTHING about my physical features or body shape that allowed me to blend into our family. Not a freakin' thing."

She sighed, squared her shoulders, "The photo in the locket…." Ashley struggled for words. "He was so handsome, your birth father. Stunning, really." And with that, the walls went up again. She stared at her hands for what seemed like hours.

"Come on, Ashley. Say something. Why did you feel like you were on the outside?"

I sat down and poured some hot coffee, wishing it were saturated with some strong liqueur. Frangelico, perhaps, with its sweet hazelnut richness.

She rested her head against the blue-striped pillows. "Because you were different, he left you alone. You're right. He didn't care about you. He favored me. But with that favoring, he told me his problems. I looked like a young, sane version of Mom. I was the substitute. He bored me hour after hour about his business and how I was to inherit his company because Mother was too drunk to manage it. He talked about his "needs" as a man she wasn't meeting. It was disgusting, Olivia. It took away my teen years, my self-image, my respect for both of them. And you, you were just the happy-go-lucky Olivia, cute, full of energy, fun, escaping day after day to school and with friends…."

"Happy go lucky? Are you crazy? I saw you as Daddy's favorite, the one he spent time with. I felt left out and miserable, afraid of him and Mom. You saw me happy with my friends, away from home. Speaking of 'away from home,' did it ever occur to you I couldn't have friends to my house and spent hours at the homes of my friends?"

I rubbed my neck. "I constantly worried what mom would be like if I brought someone home. It was embarrassing, and I tried to keep her drinking a secret."

Ashley pulled out another stick of poison. "While I…" tears puddled, "while I became Dad's dinner partner. He'd tell everyone his dear Veronica was dealing with a rare condition causing her to suffer constantly with migraine headaches. And he'd explain how he had taken her to every doctor possible for tests, to no avail. Then he'd look down, look sad for a moment or two while people sympathized with him."

She swiped at her eyes. "Everyone knew he was a damn liar. I had to smile and pretend he wasn't asshole of the year."

"Oh, Ash. I'm so sorry." I took her hand, feeling it shake. "Didn't you ever confront him?"

She paused, a look of painful memories washing over her face. "You're kidding, right?" She held the unlit cigarette between her shaking fingers. "I tried to protect you. I couldn't protect Mom. She took me aside one day, drunk, sniveling, and said Dad would start hitting me soon. And she didn't know how to stop it. But it would happen."

"And that's when you left home and lived in the dorm?"

"She told me to leave to protect myself. I couldn't take the craziness. I went to college, met Miles, got married and blocked it out…and left you alone." She stared at me, willing me to understand.

"Miles was my lifeline, my best friend, my one true love. I feel lost without him."

"Wait a minute. We're way off track here. It's something you're so good at doing, taking a twist from the subject and going somewhere else." My voice rose. "We're talking about me, my birth Father. You're making this about you. Stop it."

Ashley's mouth opened. "But…"

"I know you're still mourning Miles. But you need to stop and listen to me. I know Dad hit Mom. I know she drank. And I know why. She was an unhappy woman in a miserable marriage and living a lie. I deserved to know the truth."

"He would have hurt me if she told you the truth."

"So Mom had to choose between her two daughters? That's bull! She should have left Dad after his first affair and certainly after the second hit to the head. Stop defending her. Now! Mom drank. She was weak. She had money. She chose to ruin her life."

I stood and walked to the rail, staring at the horizon. The sea was like glass, not a ripple. I, on the other hand, felt a squall inside. Why couldn't I let this go?

"I'm not heartless, Ash. I know she fell easily into that victim mode. But I do believe it was because of her guilt over her affair that pushed her over the edge. I've carried a lot of guilt that I caused her drinking for a long time."

I turned to her, leaning against the protective rail. "Look, Ash, we're survivors. Both of us in our own way. But I can't live my life in the past anymore. I'm done. I'm moving on. I'm done excusing everyone and trying to accept what I can't change. I think I need some serious "shrink" time."

"Join the club. There's a very rich psychologist in Newport Beach thanks to me. I might have money, but it doesn't heal the hole inside me."

"Okay, Ash, here's the deal. I need to finish this."

I looked out to sea, then back to my sister.

"Mario needs closure. Mom needs to face her demons so she can die in peace."

I stood next to her, looking down and touching her shoulder. "I'm done with the drama. The only reason I came on this cruise was to meet my Father, Mario. And to honor his wish to see Veronica one more time."

Ashley raised her head, tears welling, and said, "I just don't understand."

"What could you possibly not understand? That I missed out on knowing my real Father for 35 years? That my Mother didn't have enough wisdom, courage, or love to tell me about him? That she was cruel enough to not even tell him he had a child? I guess I JUST don't understand either."

I plopped into the lounge chair and glanced at my watch. My morning gone, already exhausted, I sighed. "Get ready for your date with Anders, Ashley. I'll figure this out on my own. Just like I've always done with everything."

She pursed her lips. "That's not fair, Olivia. Why not just let Mom die in peace?"

"She'll have to make peace with all those she's hurt." I opened the slider. "You have a choice, Ash. You can live your life trying to hold all the beach balls under water. But it doesn't work. I love you. You're my sister. But right now, I can't be pulled into your dysfunctional way of dealing with life. Sorry to go psychobabble on you. But it's the truth. At the end of this trip, at the edge of the

Rialto Bridge in Venice, we are going to meet with my father. You have a few days to prepare yourself. We'll prepare Mom together."

Ashley walked away without a word, leaving me more unsatisfied than ever. I dialed for room service and ordered the drink of the day, wondering how Mario and the meeting with his wife had gone. Still burning to know if my 'father' had known about Mario, and if so, when? We got along so well until that day Ashley screamed the truth about me.

I sipped on my Rebellious Fish, served in an adorable fish bowl. Only on a cruise. The fruity concoction of liqueurs of orange, passion fruit, probably some vodka, and sparkling wine, tasted wonderful. And for a moment, I thought about ordering another. I remembered my Mom's issues and thought how tempting it was to slip into that fuzzy numbness. I pushed the thought aside, and wondered about Tony. Did he have a secret life? The signs were there. And I determined to find out more. Being attracted to him gave me hope that I wasn't completely jaded about men. I wished that Tony were here with me.

I needed Ash to understand how much I hurt. How not having a Father who truly loved me had hindered every male relationship. How having no one in my court had caused me to start building my own walls. But this conversation had managed to reveal one thing to me. Ashley, Fortress Ashley, would never understand until she decided to drop the drawbridge over the moat and face her pain.

I needed my sister desperately, and once again, she wasn't there for me. I felt an anger start to simmer.

We had to make peace with each other. Soon.

Tony

Tony felt an unusual weariness. He loathed feeling defeated.

He flipped the blue and white lounge chair to a flattened position and stretched out looking into the bright sun, clenching his fists. He'd wanted time with Olivia today, a sea day, when his clandestine activities would be minimal. His handler, however, had called for a meeting and warned him to be watchful.

Christopher was late for their "urgent" meeting, deepening Tony's black mood.

Eyes closed, lips pressed together in stress, the image of Olivia's laughing eyes danced before him, blotting out the Russian and Chinese underworld. *I must be freaking lonely. There was a spark of defiance in her, a determination mixed with humor and softness I find intriguing, even irresistible.*

"Stop it, man. Concentrate."

He checked his wristwatch and on a whim hit the speed dial for home.

"Hello, son." The soft voice of his mom gave him immediate comfort. "Where in the world are you?" she asked, laughing.

"Somewhere in the middle of the Mediterranean Sea and hungry for your pasta, Mama."

"Everything okay? You sound tired."

"Nothing's wrong, mama. I'm just a bit homesick." *Stupid forty-five-year old man calling his mom. Idiot.*

His business cell buzzed with an incoming call. Christopher.

"Just wanted to hear the sound of your voice. I'll call you in a couple of days. Love you."

"Love you, too, son. And be careful."

He grabbed the other phone. "Where the hell are you?"

"I'm in trouble." Christopher's voice was agitated. "I never made it back on board."

Tony bolted upright, almost tipping from the lounge chair to the deck. "You what?"

"You could've blown my cover today. Damn, Tony. Why'd you look at me like that? One of the guys from the crew recognized me, and ran. Some Chink saw the direction of his stare and ran straight toward me. I dumped him in an alley. And by dumped, I mean, ya know."

Tony's mouth hung open. "I barely glanced at you, shocked, by the way, to see you there. Thought you'd gone to the other side."

"Are you crazy? Tony, watch your back. Intel just confirmed the photo of the loud-mouth. He's Russian, he's Russian mafia, and he's smuggling more than drugs. He's smuggling people. Filipinos to be exact. The Bureau is cracking down on the Chinese smuggling. No one suspects crew members. The boss told me to let him go."

"How'd you miss the ship?"

"Uh, hiding a body? You didn't catch that part?"

"And you're getting back on ship how?"

"Security already checked me as a "no-show." Told me I had to fly to Santorini at my own expense and the ship wasn't responsible for my missing the boarding call."

"Shit. You idiot."

"Yeah, I know. But I'm high crew, so they were steamed but gave me a break."

"High crew?"

"I'm butler level, concierge, Tony. Don't worry about my ship cover."

Tony sighed, shrugging his shoulders. "I'll call headquarters and check in with the big guy. NeroMare will cover your expenses, you know."

"I know. I used their credit card to book the flight. See you in Greece. Oh, and don't let anyone clean your room. Call the boss NOW. Our equipment must not be seen by anyone. The cleaning staff has master keys. Stay on board tomorrow until everyone disembarks. Order room service. Keep your room secure. "

Tony slammed the phone onto the table, took a deep breath, and called Joe.

His angry voice answered. "I know all about it. I should fire his sorry ass. You need to stay on board tomorrow. Do NOT leave the ship. Christopher will follow the Ruskie. I have someone else to tail Carmella. Don't leave the room or talk to anyone until everyone is on board tomorrow night and Chris is safely in your room. We can't let anyone see that equipment."

"But I thought you wanted to let the Russian go."

"I'm in charge. You take orders from me, not Chris."

"Got it." Tony threw the phone on the deckchair. This job sucked. Stuck on this bloody ship in Santorini, Greece. Unbelievable. First thing tomorrow he'd give Vince a call. It was time to follow his dream. He placed his fingers on the side of his eyes and deeply massaged his aching temples. If he wasn't undercover, he could stop looking over his shoulders all the time.

He remembered the last visit with his best friend from college. Vincenzo. Vince to his American friends. He'd visited the vineyard and winery owned by Vince's cousin somewhere in Napa Valley. It was during the yearly celebration of harvest. Vince called it *Vendemmi*a or *Festa del raccolto.*

Tony's face crinkled with a smile remembering the pledge he and Vince had made.

"We can do this someday," said Vince, punching Tony playfully on the shoulder.

"I don't know the first thing about running an operation like this."

"I've been around vineyards my whole life." Vince had waved his arms out to the hundreds of rows of even vines. "Look at this. It's perfect. We could raise our families here."

"Whoa, Vince. Families?"

Tony opened his eyes, remembering the conversations with his best buddy. He reached for the cell, checked the time in California, and punched his stored number for Vince.

Vince answered on the third ring. "Hey, Tony. To what do I owe the pleasure of a phone call at such a bloody, inconvenient hour?"

"Hey, what are friends for? The offer still on the table to buy into your winery? Because I'm ready."

"You getting married? Awesome. 'Bout time." Vince chuckled. "You're going to love married life."

"Hold on, Fiorella. I'm not getting married. I'm ready for a job change. This one's wearing me out."

There was a pause, then a yelp. "It's gotta' be a female, right? Has to be a special woman who gives you an urge to settle down. What's her name? And what is it exactly that you do? You've never explained your job."

"It's something else."

"What's her name, Tony?"

He sighed, resigned. "Her name is Olivia. But we aren't in a relationship. Being around her just got me thinking about my dream. And, that's all it is right now."

"Whatever you say. I can't talk right now. Someone interrupted my sleep." said Vince. "Call me tomorrow about seven California time. Can you figure out how to do that, buddy? You can spill the gory details then, okay?"

"Right. Tomorrow." Tony hit the end button, a wide grin on his face.

Mediterranean Cruise
Day Nine – Port Of Santorini, Greece
Tony

Tony stood on the balcony of his suite, pounding the rail with his fists. Two days of missing Olivia. He'd seen her at dinner last night, but she appeared mellow, almost depressed, she and her sister barely speaking throughout the dinner. She'd excused herself saying she needed a good night's sleep. Gave the excuse of preparing for a busy day in Santorini.

He'd never been to Greece. And to experience it from the ship infuriated him. Especially Thira, Santorini… boasting the purest ocean water in the world. The sea sparkled, the water was cobalt blue. A volcano had severed the huge rock on which the city stood. And the bay glittering before him had unfathomable depths. Nothing but crystal clear water, clean, uncluttered like he wished his life could be.

The white buildings shimmered under the warm sun, the blue roofs like elegant hats, accentuating the starkness of the two colors. Tony sighed, surprised how the beauty affected him. He imagined Olivia strolling on the narrow cobblestoned streets and pounded the rail again.

Passengers had to be tendered to reach the shore. He watched for Olivia, but it was impossible to recognize anyone in the mass of people being crushed into the tender boats.

He hit his head with the palm of his hand. "Idiot." Then he walked to his closet and pulled out his binoculars.

His cell rang, and with a heavy sigh he answered it.

"Tony."

"Just making sure you're still on board."

"Look up. I'm on the balcony." He wanted to add a sarcastic remark, but thought better of it. "I hope you're right about this."

"Just do your job," his boss said.

"What the hell...." But he was talking to a blank phone. He threw his cell on the chair and picked up the binoculars again, focusing on the donkey trail that snaked up a steep cliff.

There were only three ways up the precipitous rocky cliffs to the tiny town perched on top of the huge rock.

Cable car, donkeys, or walking. He adjusted the binoculars to the shore and watched. To the far left, the cable cars rode up the sheer side of the rock and settled next to a white building with blue awnings. He spotted people sitting on stools along the open-air balcony drinking from small ceramic cups. He had an urge to order a cappuccino.

A few brave souls walked up the zigzagging cobble stone steps in the hot sun next to the donkeys. He focused to the right and observed a long line of cruisers waiting to be assisted onto the beasts. He could almost smell the creatures. Tiny Greek men with their traditional caps hefted each person onto a burro and walked them in groups up the narrow winding staircase, whipping the slowest animals. He moved his binos to follow the Z-formed walkway. Halfway up he spotted Christopher. Four unfortunate burros in front of him rode the loud-mouth Russian, aka Dick Yoder, who'd been causing them so much grief.

The city on the top of the rock glistened. Doorways were painted a vivid blue. Not a tree existed to provide shade.

A soft knock on his door interrupted him. He slammed the binoculars onto the cushion of his lounge chair and strode to the door.

"Good morning, sir. I have a letter." The young uniformed girl from the Purser's office handed him an envelope.

"Thank you," said Tony, handing her a tip. "Have a great day."

He returned to the patio, sat next to his morning coffee, and opened the letter.

"Dear Tony, I'd be happy to have dinner with you on your balcony tonight. I should be back on board by 5 and will call your room. Thanks for the invite. Olivia."

His face opened into a wide smile. He held the letter to his nose and inhaled her familiar scent. He picked up his Kindle and started to read, content to wait for her. He couldn't focus on Daniel Silva's new novel. His thoughts scrambled between dinner and California…Olivia and Vince. Holding the Kindle next to his chest, he silently composed his resignation letter to NeroMare, Ltd., breathing a loud sigh of relief. Undercover no more, knowing how much paperwork and red tape was required to quit the agency…he mumbled, "Gotta get out!"

Ashley

Ashley didn't like anything that made her sweat, disliked dressing down, and was appalled by bad smells. So the fact she was with Anders, who had dressed in shorts, a tee-shirt, and tennis shoes, walking toward a line to get on a donkey to climb the crooked path to the city, had her breathing deeply, feeling a slight itch on her skin. But she liked Anders. She liked his mannerly ways, his elegance in uniform, his accent, and most of all, his companionship. Without him, she might have killed her mom. Well, not really, but Anders spared her from spending every waking moment with her.

She wondered what had possessed her to insist on this trip. Living with the revelations of the past had almost undone her. She'd been pampered by her parents, then her husband, Miles. Being widowed had left her feeling afloat without an oar, a helpless female…something she detested. And the unexpected and constant battles with Olivia had worn her down. She was tired of trying to keep it all together for everyone else. She'd paid thousands of dollars to a shrink to find out why she did this only to find herself doing it again. *I'm sick.*

"Ashley, did you hear me?" Anders placed his hand on the small of her back and leaned in to her. "Are you okay?"

"Sorry. I was daydreaming." She flashed him an incandescent smile. "I'm a bit nervous about riding a donkey."

"You'll be fine. I do this every time we're in this port. Trust me."

He paid the man giving out the tickets and moved Ashley ahead of him. "I'll be here to take care of you. Really." Anders smiled confidently.

Ashley's smile was tremulous. Here she was, depending on someone to rescue her again.

"Lady, here." The small man held his hands together for Ashley to mount the skittish donkey. Ashley batted the flies away. "What's that smell?"

Anders laughed. "You look so cute when you wrinkle your face in disgust. It's donkey dung, of course."

"I don't think I can do this."

"You can."

When both of them were properly mounted, the guide led them up the first part of the hill. Ashley held her breath, feeling fear and disgust. The donkey slid on some droppings, then steadied himself.

"Look back, Ashley. It's incredible."

She turned her head and gasped. The view was breathtaking. The ship seemed like a small boat resting in the azure water. As they weaved back and forth up the zigzag steps, she began relaxing, enjoying the stunning views of the sea.

The sun beat on her back, rivulets of sweat made their way down her back, and she began to notice flies gathering on her arms and on the eyes of the donkey. A small breeze blew the smell of donkey dung toward her, causing Ashley's nose to wrinkle in disgust. She waved her hands to shoo away flies.

"You okay, Ashley?"

She laughed. "I'm fine, but the scent of these beasts is getting to me. I don't remember sweating like this before."

Anders chuckled. "You are very brave to do this. I love watching you. You have a beautiful smile." He paused. "And think how good a shower will feel. Turn around now and see how small the ship appears."

"It looks like a rowboat." She sighed. "It really is beautiful, isn't it?"

"I never tire of this view. I've sailed the world, and this is my favorite port."

Forty minutes later, they reached the end of the climb. Anders dismounted quickly and stood beside

Ashley to help her. He held her close as he lowered her to the pavement. He didn't want to let her go. Her legs wobbled.

"I need a clean bathroom."

Anders smiled. "You're glistening. It becomes you. Come on. There's a café with views that will amaze you. We'll get a cold drink."

"I can't believe I did that, Anders. Thanks for pushing me. It's an experience I'll remember forever."

Anders pulled her to him, circling her waist with his arm. "I'm glad you enjoyed it. I loved watching you. I enjoy being with you more than you know."

They ambled along the bumpy cobblestone sidewalks, passing diminutive designer shops. She stopped to look in the window at some shoes and caught a glance of her disheveled hair. Sucking in a breath, she prayed the café wasn't too far away.

They came to a large white restaurant with a blue door and walked in. The air felt cool against her skin.

"The bathroom, Anders."

"Down the stairs to your left. I'll wait."

She rushed down the winding stairwell, anxious to wash the smell of animals and sweat away. But the bathroom was tiny, filthy, and they were out of towels. She let out a shriek of irritation, and fished through her purse for tissues. She mopped her face with water, ran a comb through her hair, and peered into the broken mirror to fix her makeup. "Oh, What the heck."

Her cell rang. Her mother's number. "Now what?" she muttered. Flipping the phone open, she barked, "Hello."

"Ash, how long are you going to be gone today?"

"Why?"

"I need to finish our conversation. What if I die before I make amends to both of you?"

"You're not going to die yet, Mother. Order some food, read a book, take a nap. I'll be back about three this afternoon."

"Okay," Veronica answered weakly.

Ashley closed the phone. "Damn, now I'll feel guilty all day."

She retrieved her cell and called Olivia. No answer.

She climbed the stairs to find Anders looking refreshed but sad.

"Ashley, I've been summoned on board by the bridge. Seems some crew has jumped ship. The next tender leaves in forty-five minutes. We have time for a drink and a snack. I'm so sorry."

She shrugged. Now she had to make a decision. Stay and shop or go back to the ship and her mother. Turning to Anders, she said, "I'd like to try some ouzo." If her mother could drink to drown her sorrows, she could, too.

Olivia

I'd missed the 4:30 tender back to the ship. Now I felt rushed. I needed to freshen up before dinner with Tony.

Santorini had been crowded and hot. To add to the discomfort were four hours of cobblestones and hill climbing. And wanting to keep my feet cool, I'd foolishly worn sandals resulting in swollen, aching feet. There wasn't a level space in the city except in the stores. To take bits of relief from the hot sun, I'd dashed into air-conditioned stores… usually jewelry stores. Each time, I was hounded by owners, assuring me a good deal, a special price for a beautiful lady. Blah, blah, blah.

I swear I felt the last proprietor might tackle me on the way out. He handed me his card, promising an even better deal on a spectacular gold necklace I didn't need and couldn't afford.

"Really?" I snapped. "I'm hungry. I'll come back later." I waved and pushed the door open, willing to knock the man down if necessary.

My cell phone beeped, signaling a missed text. I knew it must be from Mario. I fumbled through my purse for the phone. Never could seem to put it in the same place twice. Flipping it open, I read the text: "C u soon. Angela difficult. *a presto. Mario.*"

A chill of dread fell over me.

But Mario's face danced in my mind, and I smiled, and the smile never went away during the tram ride down to the port and onto the tender. It lasted until I hopped onto the deck and rode the elevator to my suite.

"Ashley, is that you?" Veronica's whine said it all. My mother needed to talk.

"It's Olivia! Ashley will be back soon. I'm on my way to dinner with Tony."

"Can't that wait until Ashley comes aboard?"

"I'm sweaty and need to shower and change. I'll see you in forty-five minutes," I answered, rushing into the sanctuary of my room. Ash was supposed to have been on board at three. I wondered why she was late. I peeled off my clothes and stood in the shower, drenching my body with the soft water, emptying my mind of everything except the joy of spending time alone with Tony.

I slathered my body with the fresh scent of lemon lotion, and prepared myself for dinner. Humming. I actually was humming…something I hadn't done for a long time.

Taking a quick inventory in the mirror and liking the simple look of a crisp black sundress, I was ready to go. I peeked onto the deck and saw my mother scrunched under a blanket. It was almost ninety degrees in the sun. She was asleep, and I crept away, hoping the ding of the elevator wouldn't wake her.

Tony's suite was one floor below. I felt the heat the minute he opened the door, and the heat came from him. His smile was warm and inviting, and my heart hammered against my chest.

"Olivia, come in." he said, and took my hand. He smelled of sandalwood soap. Water droplets highlighted his dark hair. "Are we both in mourning?" He laughed pointing to his black linen short-sleeved-shirt and black shorts.

"Hey, we're Italian. Black is what we do." I followed his lead to the balcony.

"I ordered the drink of the day for you. It is, indeed, pink."

"The Pink Handgun? I saw that in the newsletter last night."

"Let's give it a try. Sounds dangerous," he said, winking. Tony took the first sip, wrinkling his nose. "A bit sweet for my taste, but I think you'll like it. It's a spunky drink. And that's what I like about you. You're spunky." Another wink.

I sipped slowly and tasted the almond and cognac immediately. I was a drinking lightweight. Needed to be careful here. I swirled the swizzle stick through the pink liquid.

"Anything to go with this?" I asked. "Empty stomach, cognac—need bread."

He walked into the room and returned with a tray of canapés. "I'm prepared. Enjoy. They're bringing dinner in half an hour, right in time for the sail away." He motioned for me to sit, and leaned back in the chaise lounge next to me. I gazed at the white buildings of Santorini, feeling relaxed. We'd been sitting there for a few minutes when Tony asked me a strange question.

"Tell me about you, Olivia? I sense mystery. The trip involves more than a family outing. Want to talk?"

He shifted in his seat and turned to stroke my hand.

I wanted to tell him everything, yet a question tugged at me. Why is he asking? And how did he know we weren't just an ordinary family on an ordinary cruise?

I took a deep breath, then another, looked into his eyes, then away. "Well…"

He leaned toward me. "Is this hard?" he said.

"Yes," I said. "But here it is. I'm the product of an affair, my father who raised me was abusive, my mother is an alcoholic, and I've met my birth father on this trip. I'm divorced, the plaintiff, it's what I call my ex, dumped me. Nutshell. Where do you want me to start?"

He touched my chin with his fingertips, a tug of a smile on his lips. "Tell me who you are. We all have our pasts. Who is the real Olivia?"

I took a large swallow of my Pink Handgun, thought for a moment, and said, "I'm a confused woman with unknown potential."

The sunrays lit his eyes, and I swear I saw them twinkle. The mouth curved into a full smile, and he laughed… and kept laughing.

"What?" I asked.

"Come here." He stood and drew me up, weightless, pressed me gently against the rail and kissed me. His lips tasted of almond and cognac. He pulled back inches, gazed deeply into my eyes, and started to laugh again.

"I love a mysterious woman. And, although I'm curious as hell about you," he paused, at once serious, "right now, all I want to do is kiss you." He pushed his hands through my hair and pulled me to him, kissing me until there wasn't enough air floating on the Mediterranean for me to breathe.

Maybe it was the good old "handgun," the pain of rejection from my ex, my mother, my life, I didn't know. I struggled between wanting to cry until there were no more tears, or give in to the sensuality of this man's delicious lips on mine. Just when I thought I couldn't take any more kissing, he stopped, gazed at me, took a deep breath, and said, "I don't want to stop."

He turned me around, leaning his back against the rail. His warm lips pressed mine. One hand slipped up my neck and into my hair. He held me and pressed his chest against mine. A headiness enveloped me, the touch of his lips were shooting through every nerve fiber until I was dizzy. And without making love to me, he absolutely made love to me for endless moments of the most physically sensual kissing of my lifetime.

I didn't notice the sound of the doorbell.

Tony pulled away, kissed my neck, kissed my fingertips, softly whispered, "Be right back," and walked to the door.

"Room service." The waiter stood in the hall, waiting for Tony to move.

"Yeah, come on in. Take it to the balcony."

"Beautiful evening for a sunset dinner, sir."

"Yes. Yes it is," said Tony, looking at me as though I were the meal.

I turned away and leaned my elbows on the railing, resting my chin on my hands, enjoying a swirl of sensations I'd never experienced. The sky was blood-orange red emblazoned with yellow. The lights of Santorini started to blink on one by one.

I felt warm arms around my waist while he nuzzled my neck. Melting, I turned around ready for anything when I heard an obnoxious voice singing an off tune version of "Wild Thing."

Tony stiffened, the smile left his face and he cursed, stomping into his bedroom to retrieve the intrusive cell phone.

"Yes," he answered. "No, I've been in my room all day." He listened for what seemed like an hour. "Could you give me some time, like an hour?" he asked curtly. He listened for the answer and threw the phone onto the bed.

The phone call had cooled him down, but I was still floating, hot. Dinner was the last thing I wanted. As much as I wanted to crawl back into his taut-muscled arms, I took his cue that maybe we should take things a bit slower.

"Tony," I said, my voice raspy with desire, "you didn't sound too happy with the caller."

"Not a big fan," he said, looking at Santorini over the gold-flecked sea, then quickly back to me. "Hey, let's enjoy dinner and the sunset." He led me to the patio table now adorned with a tablecloth and fragrant with the scents of a perfectly grilled steak dinner, pulled out my chair for me, kissed me on the back of my neck, and whispered, "We'll talk about dessert later."

Disappointment mingled with relief. I tried to relax, but every nerve in my body was on fire. I took a deep breath and made an attempt to pick up my fork and stab at a piece of romaine.

Tony talked about his dream to run a vineyard in California. I did little to further the conversation except "uh huhs' here and there, taking small bites of food. I watched him talk, took in every detail of his eyes…noticing the bright gold flecks in his dark brown eyes, the sensuous shape of his lips that had moments ago set me on fire, the strength of his hands that moved constantly in concert with his words.

We finished dinner by candlelight only to be interrupted by another phone call. Tony's face shadowed with annoyance when he returned to the table, and I knew the evening with him was over…and there would be no dessert tonight. And relief flooded me. I needed to get myself under control.

He pulled me from my chair, cradled my face between his hands and kissed me. My heart hammered again, drowning out all reason. "Tomorrow, Olivia. I'll see you tomorrow." He walked me to the door, mouthed an "I'm sorry" and closed the door behind me.

Out of breath, still stunned by the passion of our kiss, I staggered toward the elevator. I stopped against the wall, my heart still pounding.

I heard the ding announcing the arrival of the lift. Should I go to my room and hope for quiet contemplation or go to the theater for the evening's show to distract myself?

I glanced at my watch—9 p.m.—and decided– my room. Hadn't expected to be jolted out of Tony's arms by a phone call. My head told me it was a good thing. I'd been a virgin when I married Jon. And had never been with another man. Nor had I felt such desire ever with Jon as I did with Tony. I didn't want a simple fling for a physical attraction. Although, I was at a tipping point with Tony. I thought about him all the time.

Again, I wondered what he did; remembering the night in the lounge where I'd observed him and our other dinner-table guy…what was his name…Joe, John…watching people and communicating with barely a nod, never making eye contact. Yet I know they were "talking." And why didn't he go ashore today? There were more questions than answers. Was he married? What if he was into something dangerous? My heart raced for a moment. But after the romancing of his lips, I really didn't care. Quietly aroused, remembering, I walked onto the elevator and pushed the up button.

The door opened to our deck, the lights of Santorini dancing like diamonds on a necklace. The stars clustered in brightness over the island.

My cell buzzed at the same time as Ashley's voice rang out in an angry shout. "Mother, I don't want to hear it! Take it to your freakin' grave!" A door slammed. Mom wasn't strong enough for the force of that slam. Had to be Ash.

I eased into a chaise with a view toward the island and opened my cell, hoping to avoid being snagged into the middle of yet another argument.

My father's text made me smile.

"Tomorrow, 10, Sugar and Spice Bakery (Old Puca Street)."

Tension. My life was full of tension, sprinkled with tiny dashes of hope. Hope appearing when I needed it the most. Glimmers of a calmer life.

I leaned back, closed my eyes. The Greek music from the deck party below floated up happily to the top of the ship. I had been happy, too, warm in Tony's arms. I savored the memory of our short evening together, feeling his lips on mine.

The rapid clicking of heels on the deck took me out of my reverie.

"There you are!" Ashley crossed the deck to my chair in seconds, finger pointing accusingly.

"Mom is going to be the death of me. Get in there and talk to her."

She turned to leave.

"Hold it, sister. You're not going anywhere." I stood up and placed my hand on her shoulder. "What's going on? And it's time we settle this family secret right now."

Ashley turned to face me. I smelled the alcohol on her breath and saw the hurt in her eyes. I paused, trying to speak without anger. "What are you doing to yourself? Do you want to be like Mom?"

"What?" Her face reddened.

"I haven't been around you much in the last year. But on this cruise, I've noticed you drink too much. Your hands tremble. Your eyes glaze. You look confused. What's happening to my perfectly-in-control sister?"

"My life was so perfect until you came along. Everything changed. Everything. Dad, Mom, happiness, family, every damn thing in my life changed. And I don't know why."

I placed my hand on her arm. "You need to calm down. Let's talk."

"I DO NOT WANT TO TALK." Her teeth were gritted together. "She goes on and on about some affair and how abusive my dad was to her. It wasn't like that. It wasn't." Tears streamed across her cheeks and to her chin, her hands clenched at her side.

"It wasn't, was it, Olivia?"

"It was like that, Ash. That's exactly how it was."

I felt a chill of concern for my sister, realizing she was drunk and didn't remember our conversation about Mario.

Ashley shadowed me into the living room of the suite. Mother sat bundled in a blanket on the oversized couch in front of the floor-to-ceiling windows. The moon dangled in the ink-black sky, stars peeking timidly through thunderous clouds.

Veronica's blond hair was matted to the side of her mascara-streaked face, eyes watery, tiny hands clutching the top of her thick beige blanket.

"Ashley, sit next to Mom."

She eased onto the couch as if she might break Mother, and looked at her hands to avoid eye contact.

I tugged the multi-flowered slipper chair toward them, sat down, raked my fingers through my hair and took a deep breath.

"Family secrets and the inability to forgive are destructive. Mom, we need to know the truth about Dad and Mario."

Ashley's head snapped towards me. "Who the hell is Mario?"

"He's my birth father, remember?"

She sighed. "Oh, yeah. I remember."

I reached for her hand giving it a gentle squeeze. "Let Mom tell her story."

I leaned toward my mother and reached over to lift her chin forcing her to look at me.

"Are you okay? Can you do this, Mom?"

She nodded, clasping her hands together, every movement delicate…a display of fragility, exacerbated by the pain of her cancer. Her eyes looked at the wall as though searching for a window to her youth. "I'm sorry," she whispered. "I need forgiveness, but." Her breath caught in her throat. She started again, her voice weak. "I need it, but don't deserve it. Telling the truth will help me die in peace but will hurt both of you, deeply."

She straightened her back, seeming to gather strength. "All I really want is to know after I'm gone that you will be sisters who love each other and become best friends."

She glanced at Ashley. "I was a bad mother."

"No, Mom."

Veronica held up her hand to stop her.

Tears welled and spilled down Veronica's cheeks. "You look just like your daddy, Ashley. He was a Nordic god… handsome, full of life, and you inherited his beauty and some of my former beauty." She stopped, pulling her blanket tighter to her chest.

Ashley sat motionless. The tears glided down her face and onto her lap. She mumbled, "I don't want to hear any of this."

I wanted to comfort her. Instead, I handed her some tissues and asked Mom to continue.

"Eric James Andersen was at a party in Los Angeles. He'd graduated that May from USC with a degree in business. He had a gift for it: smart, cunning, brilliant 'idea' mind. Everyone who knew him said he was destined for big things, lots of money, prestige. His family, I discovered later, had made a fortune in Los Angeles real estate, gobbling up huge pieces of land in the 1940's when everyone else seemed to be suffering from the Great Depression and World War Two."

She wiped her face with her hand. "Could I have some water, Olivia?"

I walked to the glossy cherry-wood bar on the side of the room and filled three glasses, pulled some ice cubes from the ice bucket, and caught a glimpse of my tired and strained face in the reflective surface.

Ashley had not lost the shocked look on her streaked face. My heart ached for her, watching her crumble as her perfect childhood disintegrated into truth.

Mother took several sips of water, her hands shaking. She handed the glass to me and pulled the blanket tighter.

"It really doesn't matter. You both have seen his year-books, his trophies, awards, the newspaper articles showing his prowess in Los Angeles real estate. And you've both lived well from his wealth and your grandparents' trust funds. Now you need to know why the marriage was difficult." She closed her eyes, squeezing tears, grimacing from bad memories. "And why I'm a sniveling drunk."

"No one prepared me for the wedding night. My mother was silent on the subject of sex. Everything I learned was in the back seat of a car and some heavy kissing and petting. I wanted to be a virgin on my special night. I couldn't wait to put on the frothy white negligee I'd purchased. I knew Eric would love it. And he did."

She took a deep but ragged breath. "He told me I looked like an angel. His words were slurred from too much drinking. I had never seen a man naked before and it frightened me. Eric was gentle but quick, fell asleep at once, and left me wondering what all the fuss was about. I certainly didn't feel the earth move." She looked at me and smiled wanly.

"I've heard since then, of course, that it's more common than you think to be disappointed on the wedding night if you're a virgin."

She sighed. "I knew Eric was wealthy and powerful. But I certainly was unprepared for being a "corporate" wife. He was different then. But his flattery and choice of words became insulting and ugly. He became unpleasant at social functions making entertaining difficult for me. Made me nervous. Felt inadequate most of the time. Hated meeting new people. Felt a lot of pressure to look and act perfect at dinners and other social events. The more obnoxious he became, my life as the important corporate wife became intolerable."

She closed her eyes. "I just wanted to be married and have babies."

She rested her head on the pillowed couch. For a moment I thought she'd fallen asleep. Her breathing was shallow.

"Mommy, mommy." Ashley shook her gently. "Are you okay? Olivia, is she okay?"

"I'm fine." Mom opened her eyes wide. "The memories are sometimes difficult. Where was I?"

"The wedding night, Mom," I said, patting her hand to reassure her.

"Oh, that. There's nothing else to tell really. It was over quickly and the next morning Eric apologized for falling asleep."

"He drank all the time, you know." She looked at Ashley, then me. "All the time. Of course, it was for business. And naturally he needed a drink at night to help relax him. But it wasn't just one or two. It was several. He'd take me to bed, we'd make love, he'd sleep. Many times he couldn't perform because of the alcohol. And it made him angry."

"What do you mean by angry?" Ashley asked.

Mom sighed, looked at the wall again, remembering. "I was beginning to think I'd never have a child. I was desperate. The drinking became worse. I suspected drugs. Everyone seemed to be lighting up those marijuana cigarettes. I'd hear about it at the luncheons with Eric's associates' wives. All of it affected his bedroom abilities. That's when the verbal abuse started. He'd blame me. And the bedroom became a torture chamber. I felt in my heart I was barren…even frequent sex couldn't produce a baby. I made an appointment with a doctor specializing in fertility. After a barrage of tests, he pronounced there were no problems."

Veronica reached for her water glass, the blanket dropping to her lap, revealing her thinness through a gauzey nightgown. "And then the miracle. Eric came down with an awful flu. They called it the Hong Kong flu. He stayed in bed for days, ached so bad I couldn't even touch his skin. After ten days, he recovered enough to return to work. He came home happy, hadn't gone to the bar for drinks. He was on antibiotics and the doctor warned they might not work if he had alcohol."

Her smile widened. "Two months later I began to feel tired and nauseated. I was pregnant with you, my precious Ashley."

"That's when you moved to the other room." Ashley didn't ask. It was a statement of fact. "You told me he snored so loud you couldn't sleep."

"I didn't want to have sex. He lovemaking had become too rough and meaningless. My biggest fear was miscarriage. The move infuriated him, but he agreed to it until after you were born."

She gazed into Ahsley's cobalt blue eyes. "He really loved you, Ashley. You were beautiful and smart and able to charm everyone by the time you were two years old."

I could see the sweat on her upper lips and felt a sudden pity for her. "We don't need to do this anymore, Mom." I moved my chair closer to her, feeling sadness so deep my entire body trembled.

She held up her hand. "Shush, Olivia. I'll be brief." She sighed.

"Once you were born, Ash, my life was consumed by you. And, although your daddy adored you, it was almost as though now that I was a mother, he couldn't touch me. Even after I moved back into our bed, he seldom made love to me."

"One night, he came home drunk and wanted to make love. Performance was impossible. He was furious, frustrated and said humiliating things to me I can't bear to repeat."

"I took a job," she continued. "When Ashley went to school, I took a job at the small private school where Ash was a student. Eric railed at me, telling me I was an embarrassment to him. For me it was self-preservation. I insisted that I needed to be busy and would be working the same hours as Ashley was in school."

Her faded blue eyes blurred. "One day, when Ashley was I think about 10, I came home, heard Eric in the shower. I walked into our bedroom and began to hang up his suit and smelled a strong perfume. It wasn't mine. I rifled through his pockets and found a note. 'Same time, same place…you'll not be able to walk when I'm finished with you. We'll make love all night long. Jen'

"Like a piece of precious crystal dropping on a marble floor, my heart shattered into pieces."

He found me standing with the note, eyes red and swollen. He begged me to forget about it. "It's just a fling," he said. "I want things to be like they were before. A stupid mistake. We can fix this."

I looked at him, astonished. "Things weren't that good before, Eric. Not really."

He pleaded. "It's the alcohol. I spend so much time with my associates. It just happened."

"I turned away, left the room, entered the kitchen and began to make dinner. We never spoke of it again."

She turned to Ashley and spoke softly. "I began to send you home with a friend and went to the Biltmore for an after-school-hours drink. Alone. Didn't want to go home and face a husband who was, by now, openly having affairs with the flashy women in the real estate business. Free love was rampant, and women became as bold as men about affairs. What light there had been in the marriage had long since gone out."

She reached her hand to Ashley's shoulder. "This had nothing to do with you. You were loved …by both of us. So much."

I was spellbound.

"One night, a man walked into the lounge chatting with another guy, hands waving as he spoke, a smile the size of Texas. Everything about him emanated joy. His eyes were gray and flecked with gold, his hair curly and black, his skin bronzed by the sun. And when he smiled, his teeth gleamed.

He turned toward me. Our eyes locked. I stopped breathing for a long time. Had I been under water, I'd have drowned. He walked to the bar with his friend, ordered a glass of red wine and walked to a chair next to me, sat down, and told me his name.

"I'm Mario," he said. "I think you are beautiful." His accent was slight but his English perfect. He flashed a brilliant smile. "I'm from Italy. I think must be an angel."

"I slipped my wedding-banded hand under my skirt. When Mario left to bring me some wine, I took it off and put it in my purse."

He returned and handed me the glass of wine.

"Thank you," I said, smiling timidly. "I'm Veronica."

"He took my hand in his and kissed it. The gesture felt achingly intimate. A week later we became lovers, always in room 304 of the beautiful downtown Los Angeles Biltmore hotel, once a week. For six months."

Her eyes brightened. "The first time we made love, it was so exquisite, so tender, so filled with passion, I cried out in a mixture of wonder, fulfillment, relief and pure joy. Thirty-four years old, I finally experienced the beauty of making love. I didn't even know what it was. I only knew it was wonderful. And I continued to cry, experiencing a love so totally unselfish. Mario held me, whispered to me, made love to me, caressed me, and we slept naked in each other's arms all night. I breathed his scent, his skin, I clung to him."

Her faded eyes looked directly into mine. "I discovered I was pregnant. With you, Olivia." She peered into my eyes. "You were conceived out of pure love. I wish you had known your father. He never knew about you. I'm so sorry. You deserved to know him. He was called back to Italy for his mother's funeral. I was afraid to be alone, afraid of what my husband would do. So I pretended to be happy with another baby and broke off all contact with Mario." She wrung her hands. "Stupid to not even think the baby might look just like her father." She looked up, shaking her head. "Eric knew from the beginning."

Ashley cried with sobs that were long overdue. I took her hands and said, "Ashley, you're my sister, sweetheart. We need each other."

My shoulders heaved with emotion. I tried to restrain my tears, wrenching sorrow for myself, my mom, Mario, Ashley….

I turned to Mother. "I've met my father. I know him, Mother. I met him in Capri. He's wonderful."

Ashley stood up, turned toward the door.

"Stop, Ashley." I pushed myself from the chair and hugged her. "You're my sister and nothing will change that. Please, none of this is our fault. We'll work this out."

I peeked over Ashley's shoulder. Mom was smiling. It had been a long time. Mario had been the magic word.

We cried and talked for a long time. I was exhausted from the emotion and all that had taken place while in this port. Santorini delivered a day of jolting surprises: the beauty of the island, a romantic tryst with Tony, gut-wrenching confrontations with my mother and sister. My fists were still clenched even though I hoped I'd made some headway in healing things with Ashley. It would take time. My mom? I was running out of time.

The quiver from the cell phone in my pocket signaled a text from Mario. I glided across the room, stopped at my door, turned, waved goodnight to Ashley, and entered the serenity of my lavender room.

Christopher's butler skills seemed to increase each day. He'd lowered the lights in my room, turned on some easy-listening music, made a Santorini donkey out of my towels, and tucked a note in one of the ears. I plopped onto the bed, ripped the envelope open.

Dear Olivia, Tomorrow is our last sea day before Venice. Would you honor me with your presence in the private dining room tomorrow evening? I've made reservations for two at seven at "The Gondola." It's quiet, at the back of the ship with stunning views. Write a yes on this note and give to Christopher. Tomorrow, I'll imprison my cell phone in a sound-proof box. Tony. ☺

I reached for the pen on my nightstand and printed boldly…**YES!**

My phone bleeped again. I rubbed my arms, warming the chills brought on by reading Tony's note. Just thinking about being with him for an entire evening… maybe more… gave me stomach flutters and feelings that had been deadened since my ex, the good old plaintiff, had jettisoned me.

I checked the phone and scrolled to my text message.

Cara Olivia,

Enjoy sea day. Dubrovnik's, Sugar and Spice. Now read the letter I gave you in Capri. Forgiveness, Caramia. xxx

I had shivers of a different kind now. I set the phone next to my bed, padded across the flowered carpet to my closet, punched in the code to my safe, and retrieved the sealed letter Mario had given me. Glancing at my watch, I noted it was past midnight, officially when I could read the letter. The envelope screamed at me. **READ ON SEA DAY BEFORE DUBROVNIK**

Although curiosity had burned an imaginary hole in me each time I'd opened the safe, I'd kept my word and waited. With trembling hands, I slid the letter from its envelope. The more I read, the angrier I became.

Cara Olivia,

Although I speak English well, it's more difficult to write in English for me. I try. I see your eyes reflecting my regret.

*But forgiveness will heal you. Go to church, pray, make a
list: mama, papa', me, your before husband. All. You must
all forgive for the future. We talk in Dubrovnik. My wife,
I hope she forgive me – you must forgive me.
Ti voglio bene, Papa' Mario.*

Rorschach images appeared on the letter, ink smears
from falling tears. I hadn't thought about forgiving Mario.
He hadn't abandoned me. He didn't know I existed. Maybe
Mother would have been happier if she'd told the truth all
those years ago. Maybe if Mario had always been a part of
my life…. So many secrets.

I walked to my nightstand, pulled open the drawer
and lifted the Gideon Bible from the corner. I had no clue
where to begin, but I knew there were answers for me. The
index contained categories. My fingers scrolled the page
to "forgiveness." Thankfully the references had page numbers. It had been years since I'd touched a Bible.

I read through several verses. I felt nothing. But when
I found Ephesians, chapter 4, verses thirty one and thirty
two, the words seared.

*"Let all bitterness, wrath, anger, clamor, and evil speak-
ing be put away from you with all malice. And be kind to one
another, tenderhearted, forgiving one another, even as God in
Christ forgave you."*

Is this required of me to be happy? Okay. Bitter. I know
I'm bitter about the divorce. I did indeed have a smolder-
ing resentment toward Jonathan. And I seemed to hold
on to it like a life vest. I took issue with wrath. Wrath is

rage. I'm not full of rage. Anger, hostility I'll own. But I don't clamor, not even sure what that means exactly. Evil speaking – got me there. And malice, well I think I need a theologian for that one. But I knew, without Mario or the Bible, that I needed to forgive. Otherwise, I'd turn into my mother. There came the chills again. It was a chill of loneliness and dread.

My hands were getting a workout with constant clenching and unclenching. I wandered to the patio to unwind and think when my phone rang.

"Hello."

"Olivia, it's Mom. Ashley is sick. She's throwing up uncontrollably. It came on suddenly. She's put herself in isolation. I'm worried." Her voice quivered with feelings she couldn't contain. I knew she was trying to hold back tears.

"It's okay, Mom. She probably either has food poisoning or a touch of the 24-hour flu. Don't worry. Just go to bed and stay away from her until she's better, okay?"

A sniffle. "Okay. I love you, Olivia."

"I know you do, Mom. I love you, too. Now go to sleep."

I needed to comfort Mom but selfishly didn't want to be sick. That Ephesians verse should have included self-centered, selfish and thoughtless.

I walked back to the patio and inhaled deeply. As the ship moved from through the waves of the sea, the lights of Santorini were barely discernible. I breathed out in relief. Tomorrow had to be a better day. If I didn't get sick. Although Mom and I had already been exposed to Ashley. Strange, lots of people seem to have taken sick on the ship. And yet, no announcement had been made. I'd ask Tony about it tomorrow. At the thought of Tony, the pleasant chills and shivers came back. I wanted nothing more than to call him just to hear the sound of his voice.

Should I?

No. We've had this conversation before.

But just to talk.

Then he'll want to come up to see you, or meet you, or invite you to his room. Remember what almost happened last time.

I know. It was delicious.

Stay away. Concentrate on your family, Mario, forgiveness, bitterness, wrath…

Just a call.

I went back to the room and took the phone onto the patio, dialed Tony's room and waited. He answered on the second ring.

"Hello." He sounded sleepy. I pictured him in bed, hair tousled, relaxed.

"Hi, Tony. Did I wake you up?" *Stupid, stupid, woman.* Of course you woke him up.

"I was just drifting off to sleep. Are you okay?"

"I'm fine. Just had a difficult evening with the fam. You know how it goes. And Ashley is sick. She just started vomiting. No warning. Aren't a lot of people getting sick the last two days?" Great. This is one romantic conversation.

"Stay away from her, Olivia. She probably has the noro virus. And it's not fun." Tony seemed to be wide awake now.

"Olivia, did you say yes to my invitation tomorrow night?" His low voice was pure seduction.

"Of course, Tony." I wanted to say more, but my thoughts froze. I closed my lips tightly together to keep from asking him to my room.

"Sleep well, Olivia. I'll see you tomorrow night, if not around the ship tomorrow."

"No cell phone tomorrow night?" I whispered.

"No cell phone, sweetheart. No cell phone. Just me. 'Night."

Tony

He whipped out of bed and bounded to his back room. Retrieving his direct-line phone, he punched in the emergency number.

"It's the virus. That's how they're doing it. The noro virus plus something else. They're putting something in the air or the food. That's why four people have died. People don't die from the noro virus unless they're already sick and very feeble. Meet me at the bridge in fifteen minutes."

Joe, Christopher and the Captain were waiting, all grim-faced, seated around the myriad of techie instruments that guide the ship. Tony scanned them briefly, remembering his failure at technical anything in his training. Failed in language too. Sometimes he wondered how he ever got accepted into the agency.

The minute he entered the room, Joe began barking orders.

"Sit down," Joe said. "We're waiting for the doctor to meet us with the latest blood samples."

Joe glared at me. "I think you're over-reacting."

Tony rubbed the back of his neck. "Whatever. While we're all here, I need to bring up the obnoxious guy, Dick Yoder. Something about him is off."

"No kidding, Sherlock," said Chris. "He's without doubt the most obnoxious passenger on board. He's got to be undercover, but he's not inconspicuous."

"He makes his presence known," said Joe. "I'm wondering about his connection to Carmella and vice versa. We've had them tailed. Only time we got a hit on something was at a café in Naples and in Malta."

Tony stood up and paced. "I think I've figured it out. I'm going to meet with him. And call him on it."

"What the?" Joe almost leaped from his chair. He walked to Tony and pushed his finger into Tony's chest. "You'll blow your cover."

"Hey, once we figure out this mass virus thing and determine if its terrorists or just bad judgment on the part of this cruise company, I'm out."

Joe's brows furrowed, his lower teeth chewing on his upper lips. "Out?"

"Yes, out as in O U T!"

"You don't just quit the company, Tony."

"I'll take the appropriate steps." Tony turned away from Joe and wandered to the window. "I want to confront Yoder. I think he's trying to lure the crew into jumping ship and joining the underground fashion business."

He turned to face them. "I know you think the crew has a great life on this ship. But, bottom line, they're slaves. Away from family for eight months, living on tips from cruisers, acting happy and being funny to make the customers like them so they'll get more in tips. They work 12 hours a day with a half day off a week. Dead tired all the time, immune systems low, and probably susceptible to every disease possible. They probably spread the noro by never getting better, yet working anyway and handling the food, touching the silverware." He stopped for a moment, massaging his shoulders, turning his neck back and forth.

"I want to see what the Russian is offering them. Have you ever considered he WANTS to be highly visible to attract attention and gain confidence? Have you noticed the tips he gives everyone? He hands out cash like he's the candy man, and the crew members fight to serve him."

Joe chewed his lips, cracked his knuckles, and punched his right fist into his left hand as though he were hitting a punching bag. "He annoys me. I want to hit him every time I see him. Right under my nose and I never noticed. Damn!"

"Yea," said Christopher. "And Carmella is one hot babe. Every male waiter is crazy about her.

"And she flirts with all of them. Maybe she gets a kick-back from Phelps." Tony raked his fingers through his hair. "Too many things going on to distract us from our focus. I truly hate this job."

"We get it, Tony. You're lonely, you want normal." Joe's voice was threatening. "But until we are off this case, you will do your job. You understand?"

"Yes."

"Here's the doctor," said Captain Anders.

The ship's doctor, a young, thin, serious-faced family practitioner from Louisville, Kentucky, strolled in waving the paper in front of him, likely anxious to get back to enjoying the cruise he didn't pay for in exchange for three hours a day in the clinic.

"It's just the virus as I thought. The four people who died had underlying health problems. One was a severe diabetic, female, age 75; the second, an eighty-one year old woman with congestive heart failure; the third person, a seventy-year old male with advanced prostate cancer, and the fourth, an eighty-two year old man with emphysema. Most of them died due to complications from their other diseases. Their immune systems were compromised and the noro virus hit them hard. They all would have died anyway. I don't see any plot at this point. Although there was one suspicious blood test result from a fifty-year-old man whose name will be anonymous. He is in isolation for the moment.

"What I do see is a corporation not wanting to lose money. After five hundred people are sickened with this virus, it's time to take the ship out of circulation for at least three days to disinfect it, get the crew well."

Doctor Henries handed the Captain a sheet of paper. His normally calm demeanor had quickly turned to anger. "Here is a list of recommendations for this vessel. I've already faxed this to corporate headquarters. And I WILL go to the media about this if instructions aren't followed."

The Captain's face blanched as he read the bulleted suggestions.

"So?" Joe asked.

"It seems we've not been following protocol." The Captain's voice softened. "I'm going to follow up by suggesting the ship stay in Venice, docked, until it has been disinfected thoroughly."

The Captain shook the doctor's hand. "Thank you, Dr. Henries. I'll take it from here. The rest of you can enjoy the remainder of your cruise."

The doctor turned to leave, stopped, turned back and said, "Wash your hands frequently, and I'll instruct the staff and crew to wear protective gloves at all times. Including handing you a salt shaker in the dining room. And follow through or that newspaper will be alerted." He left.

"So, Boss, now what?" Tony again moved his shoulders back and forth, rubbing his neck forcefully.

"Go get a freakin' massage, Tony." Joe pounded his hand again. "We'll have a meeting tomorrow." He strode to the door, hands clenched into angry fists.

"I'm going back to bed," said Tony. But he smiled. It was dark as pitch, heavy clouds blotting out any stars. Yet he could see the sun. He saw freedom. He was thirty-eight. He could smell the grapes and the fertile soil in Napa Valley.

Olivia

Guilt is annoying, beyond bothersome. But guilt sat right down on my pillow, cuddled up next to my ear, and whispered, "Your sister is sick, your Mother is scared, and you just blew them off."

But if Ashley had the virus and Mom gets the virus and I end up with it last, it will ruin the whole purpose of this cruise for me. So with guilt hopping onto my shoulder as I got up, I plodded across the room to the portable phone, dragged my tired body onto the cool balcony and called Ash.

"Yes," she groaned.

"It's me. How are you feeling? Fever gone? Still vomiting? I'm concerned you might have the virus that's going around the ship. But I don't want to catch it. Are you okay?"

A brittle laugh. "I'm fine. Mom overreacted as always. I just ate the wrong foods today, too much red meat and some ice cream and it set off my IBS. I just won't eat anything tomorrow but toast and tea, and I'll be fine."

"Well that's a relief. I'm glad you're okay. But vomiting?"

"Yup, that's part of it. You accuse me all the time of being anorexic, but I'm thin because of this stupid condition. I call it a condition because it sounds better than a disease." A long sigh. "Can I come over?"

I glanced at the wall clock…1 a.m. "Sure. I don't need sleep."

"Sarcasm suits you so well, Olivia. I'll grab a robe and be right there. Unlock your door."

"Done. And I'll be on the patio." I stumbled to the door, opened it, padded back to the balcony and waited.

"I'm here," announced Ashley. She stumbled in attired in a short pink cotton nightgown, hair in a ponytail, looking like a hung-over teenager, and sat in the straight chair by the table, plunking a glass of juice in front of her. Without makeup, she was pale and looked weak. Looking at me with her huge blue eyes, she said, "We need to talk."

"Wow. And this couldn't have waited until, oh say, hmmm, TOMORROW MORNING? And you don't look well."

"No. It can't wait. I need to know what's going on with you. I want to advise you against getting involved with this dark-haired Adonis, and we need to discuss what to do with Mom when we get home."

I had nothing to say. I rested my head against the lounge chair, mouth open, staring at her.

"Last things first," Ashley said. "Mom. She's dying. I'd hoped we could all make amends while on this trip. Did you know, despite her illness, she's been attending AA meetings with me?"

I started to say something, but she held up her hand.

"I know. She still drinks. But she needs to make things right with a lot of people. Those meetings have kept her going the past six months. Mother has also made up her 'end-of-life' directive, signed and witnessed by me. "

She stared at me. "Are you getting this, Olivia?"

"Ummm, not really. But continue."

"When we get home, and by the way, I've taken the liberty of changing our flights, Mom will be moving in with me and hospice will be called in. She doesn't want any treatment. She presently wants peace."

She peered across the table to me. "I can see you're a bit stunned right now. Don't worry. I didn't change your ticket. You can stay for five days as planned."

I whipped my head up. "Ashley, do you have any idea how important this trip was to me…not as a bonding experience with my family…but to meet my birth father?" I stood up and moved to the balcony, staring into the calm and bottomless black sea.

"Look," said Ashley, "You're emotional, I'm practical. We see every aspect of life with a different point of view. Could you let me be the practical one right now?" She walked over to join me and slid her arm around my shoulder. "I know this is a horrible position to put you in. But when Mom sees Mario, I think the last piece of her troubled life will fall into place. She doesn't know it yet, but she needs to ask his forgiveness for keeping such a secret. It will give her peace."

"I can't let you leave without me." I wiped away a tear. "What if Mom dies before I get home? How ugly would that look to everyone?"

"Let's move past this to another subject. You and me. I'm chilly, by the way. Would you mind if we moved inside?"

I let her lead me into the bedroom where I plopped onto the bed, Ashley taking the chair. She curled her long slender legs beneath her.

"Look," I said. "I'm not in the mood, in the middle of the night, to delve into our past, sing *Kum Bay Ya*, and play nice like the last 35 years of my life are okay now that you want it to be. You left for college, married, had a rich life and left me with a bitter woman who drank herself silly every day." I punched the pillow beside me then pulled it against my chest and squeezed it tight.

"Olivia, I didn't abandon you. I grew up, and did what most kids do. I went to school and got married. I left the nest. That's what people do. And I felt terrible leaving you with Mom. Believe me, I protected you from both of them for many years." She began to twirl a loose tendril of hair by her ear.

"Both of them?"

"If Dad hit Mom, he was going to eventually hit me and you. I was his distraction. We fought all the time over you. Really, Olivia, did you think he didn't know you weren't really his daughter? He made Mom's life a living hell after she had you. One look at the dark hair and olive skin…seriously?"

"The day I remember most in my life was the day you screamed I was adopted." I squeezed the pillow tighter. "My whole world blew apart. You were hateful, and Mom brushed it off as no big deal."

"You weren't adopted." Ashley whispered. "Mom put Dad's name on the birth certificate. But you were never adopted. And the luckiest day of your life was when Dad died. He hit Mom, and sure enough he started hitting me, and if he hadn't died, he would have hit you."

Ashley crawled onto the bed beside me and brought my head to her shoulder. "I love you, Olivia. From the day you were born, you were my little baby doll. But you could really get me angry. Our differences caused clashes. I was closed and proper like Mom and tried to live up to Dad's expectations. You were carefree and happy, always the clown, always approachable. I was filled with jealousy. Especially when Mom defended you against anything and everything. Now I know it was because she really loved your father."

I nestled my head deeper into her shoulder. I began to shake and the tears came. They wouldn't stop. My sister held me closer, whispering, assuring me everything would be alright. She'd be there for me. From now on, she'd be my older sister, someone to depend on for love and support. I kept crying until the tears ran dry.

I woke up still in Ashley's arms. It was now four in the morning on the wall clock. I stirred.

"Olivia, are you okay?"

"Hey," I answered, my voice raspy from the cry, my nose stuffed. "Why wouldn't I be okay? I know the whole ugly truth now." I rolled over and reached for a tissue on the nightstand and blew my nose. "I do feel better about us. And I know there's so much more you need to tell me. But we have the rest of our lives to deal with that. Thank you. Want to move right on to Tony, now?"

Ashley smiled. "I think you've had enough sisterly advice for now." She tucked her fingers under my chin. "But I'll say this. You are not over your divorce yet, nor are you over Jon. I am begging you to not make the same mistake I did. Don't go hopping into bed with someone you barely know because it feels good."

She patted my hand. "We'll talk about it later."

I rubbed my puffy eyes, squinted and said, "Will you forgive me, Ashley?" *Where the heck did that come from?*

"Of course. I think we need to discuss this more. But we will all forgive each other and start fresh." She paused, leaned over and kissed me on the forehead. "When Mom is gone, I promise, we will be the best sisters ever. The very best. Now I need to get some sleep."

I must have slept like the dead. I heard the faint ring of a phone. But I couldn't move. Opening one eye, I stared into the bright sun. After the usual questions of 'where am I and what time is it' I managed to roll over and look at the clock. Noon. I bolted upright. What the heck? Then I remembered my middle of the night soirée with Ashley. It seemed unreal. Phone rang again. This time I reached for it and uttered a groggy hello.

"Hi, beautiful. Remember me? We have a dinner date tonight?"

Tony. Crap. What had Ashley said about Tony?

"Hi, Tony. I'm still in bed. Was up half the night." I yawned into the phone. Not cool.

"How's your sister?"

"She's fine. Turns out she had an attack of IBS that put her down. But she's fine now." I stifled another yawn. "Tony, I just woke up. Let me call you later. I need to spend some time with my sister and Mom this afternoon."

"Not a bad idea to stay away from crowds of people. Wash your hands constantly, don't touch handrails, use a tissue to push any elevator buttons, and…just be cautious."

"Tony, I really want to spend the evening with you. But no expectations from me? Okay? I'm not a prude. But I need to be cautious."

"I love spending time with you, Olivia. Don't give it another thought."

"Bye, Tony."

"See you for dinner tonight."

I hung up the phone feeling like a gawky teenager who'd just put on a chastity ring. He probably thinks I'm an idiot. Maybe I am.

I reached for the phone and dialed Ashley's extension. She answered on the first ring. "Hi, Sis. Christopher is bringing brunch. Ready to eat?"

"Just make sure he brings lots of coffee. And, thanks, by the way, for ruining what could have been a very romantic evening with a gorgeous man."

"See you in a few." She hung up the phone.

"I'm doomed with men. Just doomed." I trudged into the bathroom to take a shower. I knew I was in for a difficult afternoon with the family. I also knew my sister was one hundred percent right. I could not even think about a relationship with Tony until I found out who is really was…and resolved the issues with my mother and sister. I also knew I'd finally let go of Jonathan. He was my past. I had a new family in Italy who were my future. And, although the relationship was new, I had hopes Tony might be a part of the future too.

Angela And Her Daughter, Mia (In Venice)

Angela drummed her fingers on the kitchen table, stopping periodically to sip her latte. She'd tried to tame her wild blond curls with a rubber band and pins, attempting to make a tight knot atop her head. Tendrils of curls had been coaxed free by the humidity and swirled around her face. Even devoid of makeup, she belied her age.

"Mama, please. Talk to me. And stop furrowing your brows. You'll get wrinkles."

Angela's mouth tightened. "You insult me?" she asked, breaking the silence. "And expect me to talk."

"Mama, stop this nonsense." Mia pushed her wayward dark curls from her glistening face. "And turn on the air-conditioning. It's hotter than hades in here."

"You know how I feel about air-conditioning, Mia." She continued to drum her fingers, slower now, in deliberate thumps of anger.

"This isn't about the AC, Mama. This is about all the years of marriage to Papa' and now making him suffer for something that happened 35 years ago. Thirty. Five. Let it go. Forgive him."

Angela looked at Mia, eyes glistening with tears. "It's not about the 'mistake' or even Olivia." She reached across the table for Mia's hand. "It's about the woman. What if he sees her and remembers, remembers something they had that we could never have?" She pulled at the edge of the table cloth, twisting it, looking out the window onto the beauty that is Venice. "Or has regrets, or loves this Olivia more than he loves my children? I never knew another man. Only your father."

"Mama, I've met Olivia. Except for the age difference, we look like sisters. She's nice and quite nervous about all of this. I wanted to not like her." She pushed her chair back, and walked around to her Mama. Putting her chin on Angela's shoulder, she said, "You cannot erase all these wonderful years of a loving marriage. Nor can you erase the fact Olivia exists. It's a blip in your life. She won't live here. Her life is in California. Be the bigger person."

A span of silence stretched between them.

"I'm ashamed of how I treated her when we had lunch," said Mia. "Very ashamed."

Angela reached up to stroke Mia's hair. "Let's go onto the patio and talk. You can tell me what she's like, how she is with Mario."

Mia grabbed a bottle of water and two glasses and followed her Mother onto the shaded patio, both settling into the plush yellow chairs.

"I mean it, Mama. You have to deal with this or you will make everyone take sides. You'll destroy Papa's relationship with his children. And you'll just become bitter. Where's that fireball Daddy married? Please?"

"Where did you sneak off to meet this Olivia?"

"I didn't sneak. I went with Papa' on a business trip to Taormina." Rolling her eyes, she said, "And stop calling her 'this Olivia.' She is simply Olivia. And she's innocent in all of this."

"So this Olivia, I mean, Olivia, she looks nothing like her Mama?"

"You'll be shocked. I told you, we look like twins except for the color of our eyes." Heat suffused her face. She blotted her neck with a napkin. "But she is gentle like Papa'. And I'm temperamental like you." She managed a weak smile, hating to admit she was so much like her aggressive and spirited mother.

"Mia, I cannot show weakness. I will not simply give in to my husband and be all nice and sweet. "

"Nice and sweet isn't you, I agree. But Papa' has suffered enough."

"What do you know of this other woman, this Veronica?" She reached for her water, holding the sweating glass next to her neck to cool her. "How does he talk about her?"

"He doesn't say much. Just wishes he'd known about Olivia." She left out how her brothers probably knew more and had shrugged their shoulders.

"You know the boys. They want to make sure the future of the business and the money stays in the family, OUR family. Other than money, I don't think they feel one way or another about Olivia." Mia frowned. "But they don't want you hurt. If you will just stop making Papa' miserable, make an effort with Olivia, and tolerate Veronica, everything will smooth out."

Mia leaned in and took her mother's hand. "You don't have to meet Veronica. But I will tell you this. Olivia's relationship with her dying mother is not good. Her cancer is advanced. This was supposed to be a healing trip emotionally for the three of them."

"Three of them? You mean there's another child?" She pulled the band from her hair, pulling it to the side and worrying strand by strand, the storm clouds gathering in her eyes.

"Mama, no. Veronica had her first child by her husband." Mia stood and pulled her Mother from the chair, hugged her, and soothed her like a child. "Everything will be okay. Yell at me. Scream. Call Papa' every name you can think of. Pound something, anything. But for the sake of the family, forgive Papa' tonight when he comes home."

Angela took her glass and threw it against the wall, shattering pieces of glass over the patio.

"Feel better, Mama?"

"No. But I will. Now clean that up." A smile edged the corner of her lips. "I love the man." She shrugged. "And when we all meet, that woman will see how much he loves me. Stupid woman."

Mia walked to the kitchen, took a deep breath, gathered a broom and dustpan and returned to sweep the broken glass. She found Angela leaning against the balcony, humming.

Mia shook her head. *Dear God, help me to not be so much like her.*

Mario

Mario sank back into the blue canvas bench, resting his head, watching the seagulls and pigeons battle for food from the liquid highway known as the Grand Canal. He gazed at the magnificent church of the *Santa Maria della Salute* across from the canal and pleaded with God to calm the hearts of everyone. He needed to think, plan, even plot his way back to Angela's heart.

He'd even been willing to enlist the help of his daughter, Mia, who most likely was trying to convince her Mother to accept Olivia. He knew Mia wasn't exactly thrilled about this newfound sister; she had made her unhappiness quite clear. But she'd agreed to try anything for peace in the family and to calm her Mother's rage, which had been turned inward into a very long and painful silent treatment.

Mario had tried to the core of his being to make her understand this wasn't about Veronica. He just needed closure, to know Veronica was okay, to get some questions answered for him and to protect Olivia.

"*Espresso, Signore.*" The waiter placed his coffee on the polished cherry table.

"May I have some water, please?" Mario's lips and throat were dry. Olivia would arrive in a few days. He had to have this settled.

The canal water lapped against the bobbling gondolas. Despite the Venetian name for the city, *Serenissima,* clear, bright and fair, the last two weeks had ground slowly, anything but serene. He thought about his life. For the most part it had been gentle....with an occasional storm capsizing him over at times. But he'd weathered the up and downs, finishing law school, working with his father in the law firm of Carapelli, Carapelli, and D'Angelo, learning corporate law and specializing in import-export.

In law school, he'd met Angela. He'd fallen immediately for her Venetian look, volumes of blonde curly hair, and eyes so green and brilliant...he'd been hypnotized by them. She'd come from old money inherited in part by royalty in the family and a lucrative glass-blowing business. Their home, passed down from generations before, was stunning. Angela insisted she would have to live there when she married.

"Angela, I want to provide for you. Please."

But she came from a stubborn family of privilege, and her father sternly insisted the house would be part of her dowry.

Asking for her hand in marriage had been the most frightening thing he'd been required to do in his young life. They were the perfect couple, saving themselves for marriage, heavily chaperoned by the family. Signore Caputo had hoped for a suitor with more money. His daughter, however, was determined to marry for love. Happily, the families had grown close.

When Angela had walked down the aisle of the church he was now facing, she'd literally taken his breath away. It seemed like yesterday when he stood at the altar and watched as the families came in, all of them smiling. And then Angela appeared with her mother and father. She was covered from head to toe in white, her gown a simple satin, clinging to her body, her shoulders hidden by a lace veil that seemed to trail the entire length of the church. Bouquets of white roses blanketed the altar, and in the aisle each row from the back of the church to the front was adorned with clusters of rosebuds and baby's breath. After the ceremony, the wedding party and their families rode in four gondolas to the reception area in the Piazza San Marcos in a ballroom of Hotel Danieli. The reception was elegant yet traditional with dancing and music and the money dance. Money had been pinned on every inch of their clothing. They'd laughed and laughed when the money had been counted. Over ten thousand dollars, enough to pay for a glamorous honeymoon on the French Riviera…Nice, and Monaco.

They'd been so happy. Over the years, he'd learned how to get around her tantrums. He remembered one evening when he'd come home late. She'd made a romantic dinner, candles had been placed on the dining room table, and he had forgotten to call her to let her know he'd be late. He'd gone out for drinks with friends from work and arrived home perfumed with wine and cigar smoke. Angela was furious. She'd lost her temper, slammed the door to their bedroom shouting, "Eat dinner by yourself."

He'd quietly cleaned the kitchen, ate a few bites of the delicious veal, packed the rest in the refrigerator, and then blew out the candles. He'd knocked on the door.

"Go away."

He had also learned to leave her alone after her temper flared and knew by tomorrow she'd be gentle as a lamb. And she was.

The dreaded silent treatment had been the most effective in her arsenal of tools to get her way. He remembered one time when he'd broken a promise to take her to Paris for their tenth anniversary. She'd exploded, then pouted for days, not caring that he didn't have the money at the time. Theirs was a passionate marriage in every way, in the bed, the laughter, family time, and fights. Everything in the extreme.

But Veronica had kept a small part of his heart and mind. He knew she was a fantasy, a fling of the past. But she'd captured his soul. Or had he just been young and foolish, free from the prying eyes of the family? Not yet married, wondering if there was something more out there. And then that night in the bar of the Biltmore…the fragile Veronica and his homesickness caused him to lose his way. He knew it was wrong the first time he took her to bed. She was an addiction, an American with different ways, not surrounded by propriety. Fun and carefree. Older than him. But a baby? Why hadn't she told him?

"She's dying and she's an alcoholic. She's been a terrible mother. The woman you loved is not the woman I've known all these years."

Olivia's bitter words had stunned him. He gulped his espresso, sipped his water, and speculated again if he was the cause of her change. Guilt followed him like a storm-filled cloud. Did I destroy everyone? Veronica, Olivia, and now my Angela?

With a sigh, he paid his bill, got up and walked to the railing. The church's imposing face topped with the disciples and other church figures glared at him, the evening sun hitting the marble and shooting back at him as if a rifle aimed its laser sight, leaving a bright circle on his heart. Church. He wandered from the hotel, down the street, and turned into a narrow and unlit dark alley to the water to fetch a gondola.

He crossed the canal, and unsteadily placed his foot from gondola to pavement, striding with deliberate steps to the front of the church. He entered the hushed sanctuary, crossed himself with holy water, and headed to the nearest confessional.

He entered, sat, sighed, his mind conflicted with words of confession. A soft rustle. The curtain parted.

"Yes, my son. How may I help you?"

"Forgive me, Father, for I have sinned."

For thirty minutes he sobbed and told his story, the priest waiting.

"Forgive yourself," the priest said, his voice gentle, quiet. "Then beg forgiveness from all you've hurt."

"What else? How do I atone for this sin?"

"You've atoned through suffering and confessing. Now you must confront. God will help you on your journey of healing. Go and God be with you, in the name of the Father, Son, and the Holy Spirit, Amen."

Mario reached for the freshly ironed handkerchief in the pocket of his jacket, and wiped his face. He knew what he had to do. He didn't know the outcome, but he'd do what was right in the eyes of God. His step was lighter, his fear diminished.

He hurried from the church to his home. Consequences were a natural part of life. But his confidence level had increased. His faith in his love for his wife was strong. He paused at the front door, breathed deep and started the climb up the many steps to the penthouse.

"Angela, I'm home." He inhaled the aroma of crushed garlic, basil, pine nuts and the pungent scent of Parmigiano Reggiano the moment he opened the door. She was cooking his favorite meal. Pasta with homemade pesto. She still made it the old-fashioned way by crushing the ingredients. He walked into the kitchen.

"Ciao, caramia. It smells wonderful in here." He strolled up behind her and wrapped his arms around her waist, leaning in to nuzzle her neck. She smelled of olive oil and basil, clean and intoxicating.

"Still not speaking to me?" He kissed her neck again.

"Of course I'm speaking to you, you fool." Her tone of voice had gentled.

He took her shoulders and turned her to face him. Dried tears streaked her face.

"Che cosa?" Mario thumbed her cheeks, gazing into her eyes, now a soft green. "Why the tears? I love you and only you. We have a wonderful marriage and family. Come with me. I need to say something."

Mario led her to the living room sofa where they sat close to each other. He turned to her and took her face in his hands. "I'm so sorry. I've hurt you. I feel so much guilt. Will you please forgive me?"

Angela looked away and whispered, "I forgive you." Her shoulders rolled forward and back to release tension. "I will meet this daughter. I will meet this woman. I will be nice to this Olivia. I cannot promise you about the woman."

Mario pulled her into his arms. They sat in this embrace, Angela crying softly.

Finally she pushed him away, her eyes taking on that stormy look that gave him pause. "Was there anyone else?

After we married? Because if there was, you will pay for the rest of your miserable life."

Mario chuckled. Angela was back. This Angela he could handle. The silent Angela brought him only misery. "You are my one true love. Foolish woman." He kissed her, feeling a desire for her so intense it shocked him.

Her breath ragged, she pushed him away. "The pasta water is boiling."

"Forget the pasta, Angela. Forget everything but us." He led her to the bedroom and slowly undressed her, enjoying every contour of her body. He saw the desire in her eyes. She moved to him, unbuttoned his shirt, kissed his chest,

"It's been too long." She pulled him to the bed and kissed him with the same hungry passion of their wedding night and all the years since.

Later, their bodies spooned together, Angela whispered, "Was she good in bed?"

"*Mannagia*, Angela. Let it go! And, no. You have a passion most men would envy. Now let me sleep. I'm exhausted." He held back a chuckle. Maybe a little jealousy wasn't so bad after all. He closed his eyes and fell into a deep satisfied sleep.

He awoke the next morning feeling more rested, more alive, and extremely satisfied that his love and marriage with Angela still held intense passion and joy. He knew the coming day in Dubrovnik would be tense, difficult, and other emotions he didn't want to think about if Angela went along with the crazy plan he'd concocted.

He glanced at her, sleeping peacefully next to him, her hair fanned against the pillow in the morning sun, beams of light reflecting the gold strands in her hair. She was angelic in sleep. When awake, you never knew who she might be. But it kept their marriage exciting.

He'd formed a scheme, knowing it was dangerous, maybe foolish. But he would propose it to his wife today. He was prepared for the anger, or maybe the silent treatment. He'd had many years of these reactions. He smiled, fortifying himself even now. She'd come to agree with him. It would just take a couple of days of complete misery, but all would be good in the end.

She stirred, puffing out little breaths, rolled to her side facing him. Her eyes popped open. Mario leaned on one arm and with his other reached over and stroked her face.

She bolted upright. "What do you want, Mario?" Her green eyes darkened as she gave him a calculating look.

"Want? I'm just enjoying looking at you." He leaned in to kiss her.

"Stop." She held out a hand, her brow furrowing. "You're trying to soften me up for a hare-brained scheme dealing with Olivia, aren't you?" She flung the sheet off, kneeling over him. "What?"

Mario sighed. He sat up, drawing his knees to his chest. "*Caramia,* please. Just listen. We need a holiday, right?"

Angela's expression didn't change. The only difference was the pursing of her lips.

"Just listen. I have to go to Dubrovnik for business and will meet Olivia there. I thought we could go together; spend a couple of days in the old city."

Angela's mouth hung open. But she remained silent.

Mario kept talking. "It would be romantic. You wouldn't have to meet her, just observe her while we have a coffee." He paused, watching for a reaction, afraid to touch her.

The silence seemed eternal.

Angela moved from the bed and padded across the tiled floor to the wardrobe, opened it, flung her flimsy white night-gown on the bed, barely missing Mario's face, and pulled a blue cotton shift over her head. Without a word she marched to the bathroom to brush her teeth. When she came back into the room, she'd brushed her hair back from her face and pulled it into a ponytail. She didn't glance at her husband.

She's giving me the silent treatment. He shrugged. *Better than a temper tantrum.* Mario flung his feet to the floor and strode to the side chair to retrieve his jeans. He strolled cautiously into the kitchen to find Angela sitting at the table, face in hands, silently weeping.

He moved toward her, pulled the chair back, and pulled her up to his chest. "Angela, please don't cry."

"I love you, Mario. I love my family. You know family is everything to me. Everything. Now these intrusions this late in my life. It's unbearable."

He took a deep breath. "If it's too much to ask, you don't have to go with me. I thought it might make it easier if you just see her."

"It's Veronica. It's her I don't want to see." Her voice quivered, tears streaming down her face. "It's always been you and me since I was a young girl." She looked into his eyes. "You understand?"

He pulled her close. Murmuring softly, he reminded her Veronica was dying. "Veronica is a memory of long ago. You are my only true love. But forgiveness, Angela. I have to have her forgiveness."

"But she kept such a secret from you. It was wrong."

"And what would she have gained by telling me, really? Angela, she spared me from ruining our relationship. Times were different. People looked at things in a different way, especially in Italy."

"I understand. But she hurt Olivia." She buried her face onto his bronzed chest and wept.

"It's okay, Angela. Whatever you decide is fine with me. You don't have to go with me to Dubrovnik. It was just one of my crazy ideas. I'll go alone, talk with Olivia, prepare her as best I can for meeting the family in Venice." He lifted her face to his and kissed her with as much tenderness as he could.

"I'll go with you," she said quietly. She sighed. "'I'll go and see this daughter of yours. But I won't meet her yet. Now sit. I'll make your coffee." She glanced slyly over to him. "You must be hungry. I had to get up and put the pesto away. Want it for breakfast?"

Mario laughed. "Sure. I'll start the pasta water. And I'm starved, you're right. But, Angela, you filled me last night with wonder. I slept like a baby." He winked at her.

She walked to the stove to start the espresso. With her back turned to him, she said, "And I will do a lot of shopping in Dubrovnik. A lot."

Mario smiled. "Anything you want, my angel. Anything you want."

Day Ten – Sea Day
Tony
Cabin Number 1174

The safe room in his suite was body-heat stifling. Joe's beefy build seemed to expand in the tiny room. Joe and Tony hovered around the computer.

"Tony," said Joe. "Where are you? Because you're sure as hell not here! We need to wrap this thing up now." He squinted at the computer screen, shoulders hunched, arm muscles taut, biting the inside of his cheek, Clydesdale hands flying over the keyboard. "This whole undercover mess could have been solved by a rookie. None of this cloak and dagger stuff. Sometimes, since 9/11, everyone reacts like a hair-trigger on a gun."

Tony nodded. "Well, what do they call it? A mission creep? We're here for one thing and others are here for something else. It's a freaking waste of time to follow someone who isn't part of the deal. I want out. I want out of covert operations. In fact I want out of NeroMare Limited. I'm quitting."

Joe looked down, frowning. "Go for it. Your decision. Remember, you can quit, but you can't leave."

Joe turned his pudgy face to Tony. The scar on his temple whitened, standing out like a streak of lightning. "You're one of our best. Think about going overt instead before you put in your notice. Three more years and you're pensioned out." He scratched his face in frustration, pounding on the computer keyboard, trying to find the information he needed to close the case. "Bloody waste of everyone's time."

He furrowed his brow. "Aha. Here it is." He pointed to the form on the computer screen. He stood up, holstered the gun sitting on the desk, and said, "Fill out the paperwork for this job." He cracked his knuckles and continued typing. "I'll get you off the ship in Venice. You have a week to get back to headquarters in Virginia to complete your transfer out."

Joe glared at Tony. "Think long and hard. You've got a broom up your butt with this woman. Go get laid, get rid of some frustration. If nothing else, remember what your full retirement pay will be. And we're not broke like those government agencies."

Tony tensed, ready to explode. "It's not the woman. It's the job." He turned toward the door, wanting to head for the balcony, but knew the place had to be secure before he could leave. "I'm definitely attracted to this 'woman,'" he said. "But that's not it. I finally have a chance to follow my dream. And it isn't following Russians and Chinese or any other underworld people. They can all kill each other. I want a chance at normal. And my buddy has given me that chance… to own a vineyard in California."

He sat down at the computer to fill out his paperwork. "And I miss my family."

"Whatever." Joe tugged on his sports coat, his arm muscles so big, they seemed about to pop out the seams on the sleeves. "I'm going to see ship security and sign off with the Captain." He glared at Tony. "Good luck."

He opened the door and paused. "Clean and secure the damn room, pack it up. You know where to put everything. One of our guys will store it for shipping in Venice. He's already cleared to board the minute customs clears the ship. See you at NeroMare headquarters. I'm flying out from Dubrovnik tomorrow." He paused, shrugged his shoulders, mouth tightened into a straight line. "Don't blow your cover. It'll cause a stir with the crew. Be the good guy. Try to convince them, the ones you know who're vulnerable, to not jump ship. It's not a good choice for them."

Joe slammed the door of the cramped room on his way out.

"Hate it when he's in a nasty mood, but he's the best handler I've ever had," Tony said, talking to himself. "Still want out. Out completely." Yet, he thought of the very generous pension he was about to give up. And wondered if there was a way.

He worked on securing and packing the equipment, turned back to the keyboard and entered the necessary data about the mission, the outcome, filled in the required forms. When all the proper documentation was completed, he hit 'send.'

With a heavy sigh, he focused on dinner with Olivia tonight, whispering to himself, "I can change."

Olivia
Garden Villa Suite

It's a mistake. I kept thinking my plans for tomorrow were a terrible crisis just waiting to happen. Ashley in Dubrovnik with my birth father? I buried my head in my hands, thinking about seeing Mario tomorrow and my dinner date tonight with Tony. Ashley was right, of course. I couldn't just hop into bed with him. I had too many family issues, I'd feel guilty, and I certainly didn't need a relationship right now. In fact, the only relationship I needed to concentrate on was with Mario and his family—my family.

The butterflies in my stomach rumbled with each other.

I gazed at the glass-smooth sea, trying to calm my nerves.

"Olivia? Olivia, are you on the balcony?"

"No, Mom. I'm out here on the deck by the pool. What do you need?"

Veronica padded out the door and over to me. She looked like a waif from a refugee camp, frail, facing starvation. "Mind if I sit here with you?"

I patted the chair next to me. "Sit down. I'll get you a cold drink. Water, soda, ice tea?"

"Actually, a wine spritzer sounds good. Lots of ice."

"Mom…"

She waved her hand. "I know I'm not supposed to have alcohol with my meds. For the love of God, I'm dying anyhow. What difference does it make?"

"You're right." I walked to the bar, pulled out some white zin, some seltzer water, plunked in the ice and served it up. "You should eat and drink whatever you want at this point. I agree."

She lifted her rheumy eyes toward me and smiled. "Thank you, dear."

She drank it like she'd been stranded on a waterless island for days. I walked back to the bar and made another. If she didn't care anymore, what was the point of following doctor's orders? I just wanted her to live long enough to get home and die in peace.

"Honey?"

"Yes, Mom."

"What are you doing tomorrow in Croatia?"

I felt deep sadness thinking about her and Mario and how an event so long ago could change a person's life.

"You're too weak to get off the ship, Mom. Ash and I are going into town for a couple of hours. You need your rest for Venice. We'll have one day there and then you fly home." I took her blue-veined hand in mine and stroked it. "Just rest today and tomorrow. I love you, Mom. You know I do."

"I've been a lousy mother. I know that, Olivia. I thought I did my best. But, as I look back, I was so very very selfish. So many regrets," she whispered. "So many."

I took her hand in mine, but her eyes were closed. She'd drifted off. I gazed at her drawn face trying to remember the beauty once there. I remember seeing a photo of Lucille Ball in her earliest movie. How gorgeous she was. I tried to imagine my mother when Mario first met her. But too many bad memories had marred her beauty for me. I leaned over to kiss her forehead. "I love you, Mom. I forgive you."

But it was too much. I looked at my sleeping mom and wept.

Day Eleven – Dubrovnik, Croatia
Olivia

The view from the balcony was a quilt of blues, sapphire sky against the brilliant deep aqua sea. Emerald fir trees stretched lazily from the jutting rocks. The old walled city peeked over the port displaying dazzling red-tiled rooftops. Everything glittered in the warm morning sun promising a picture-perfect day in Dubrovnik.

While sipping my coffee, I thought back to the midnight conversation with Ashley. She'd been so sick from what we thought was the virus, her body warm, her face flushed. Thinking about life without her had obliterated any resentment. I needed my sister; she needed me. We'd talked nonstop, rehashing old hurts, and good times, and memories long buried, both good and bad.

With a deep breath, I relaxed my shoulders, relieved at how three words could change a life forever.

"I forgive you," I'd said.

"I forgive you, too," Ashley had responded.

We'd stood by the rail holding each other, crying, trembling with emotion and relief at the shedding of years of bitterness. Time seemed to melt away, taking us back to happier days and memories of an innocent time.

For the first time on this cruise I felt happy. And relaxed. My father had been right all along. Forgiveness is the key to healing yourself. And I couldn't wait for my sister to join me for a day in this port.

I'd invited her, on impulse, to meet my Italian Papa', and she'd accepted, breaking down again in tears.

I leaned back, enjoying the mosaic of contrasting colors that paint this historic city and its shores. When the phone rang, interrupting my reverie, I didn't jump…another sign I was relaxed.

"Good morning."

"Good morning to you."

"This is a pleasant surprise, Tony. What's happening with you today?"

"I have some business in Dubrovnik proper." He paused. "Olivia, I really want to meet you in Old Town today. The ship departs at ten tonight. The views are spectacular at sunset."

I could feel my heart pounding. "I have plans today with Ashley. And we've arranged for a staff member to take

Mom for a little outing." I closed my eyes, trying to finagle a way to meet him. "How 'bout we text about four this afternoon. I should be free by then."

"I have a secret place to take you for the sunset. Never been there. A recommendation from a friend. Please?" He asked, in *sotto voce.*

Did he practice this voice over the phone, or was it just naturally sexy? "Believe me, Tony; I really do want to meet you. But things are complicated today. I'll tell you about it one way or another, at your 'secret place' or on the ship."

"Don't disappoint me, Olivia. It'll be worth it."

"Okay." But I'd answered an already finished conversation. He had a habit of just hanging up without waiting for a response. I wondered if it was an MO for his job, or a bad habit. If I did see him this evening, I was going to try to discover why I felt there was something clandestine about him. Added to the sexual tension for sure. But again, I had to wonder if he was involved in something sinister.

Phone rang again. This time it was Ashley. "Hi, Sis."

"Hi, Olivia. Had a time with Mom about us leaving her for the day. She's feeling so weak, I feel guilty. Christopher assured me she'd be well looked after and repeatedly reminded me we are only a phone call and ten-minute ride away. Assure me, Sis."

"I'm assuring you. You need to meet Mario so we can plan a strategy for reuniting them. They need to forgive each other, too. Well, you know, like we discussed."

I heard a loud blow of breath from Ash. "Okay. What time?"

I glanced at my watch. "I have to meet Mario at eleven at the Sugar and Spice Bakery on Old Puca Street. Meet me at the disembarkation ramp at nine. And, Ash," I whispered. "Thanks."

Another huge sigh echoed into the phone. "No problem. I'm looking forward to the day with you."

I rushed to get ready, still wanting to look my best when meeting my new-found Father. I spritzed my hair and crunched it to enhance the curls, checked my makeup, and dabbed some perfume on my wrists and throat, grabbed my purse, and headed for the elevator.

"Wait for me," said Ashley, running after me. "Surprised you, huh, being ready on time?" She smiled.

She looked so perfect and beautiful I almost reverted to the 'jealous of how gorgeous she is compared to me' thought, and then remembered how much it didn't matter anymore.

We entered the elevator together and queued with other passengers, slid our identification through the machine and hurried down the ramp, continuing to avoid the pushy ship photographers.

The ship had arranged to take passengers from the port to the city gate via a trolley. The contrast of beige walls and the blue of the sea took our breath away. We stood for a few minutes soaking in this unique sight. The walls were still scarred from the war, cracks and holes where bullets had passed through. But other than that, Unesco had done a great job of preserving of this walled city.

We wandered down the main stone-covered streets. There were no vehicles allowed and our shoes echoed off the beige bricks. Some of the shops had modern doors and windows with designer clothes displayed. Others had the original windows, small and grated with narrow entrances and unfamiliar merchandise. We continued in comfortable silence, something new for me and Ashley. It felt good.

"You look like you belong here, Ash. Look at all the tall blondes in the shops."

"I noticed. But look at the Slavic cheekbones." She sighed. "Aren't you nervous?"

"I've met Mario three times on this trip. Capri, Florence and Taormina. I can't wait to see him. But I should have warned him I was bringing you along." I glanced at her. "You look so much like Mom when she was young."

"Right. I look like her, but I'm not 'like' her. Right, Sis."

I patted her arm, smiled, then pointed to a steep set of narrow stone stairs. "Let's explore. We have thirty minutes to kill."

We peeked into the shops on each of the three levels, giggling like real sisters. I made a mental etching of this special time. I knew we would be in for drama when we docked in Venice.

Our map from the ship presented us with Croatian street names…and Old Puca Street wasn't one of them. We spotted an older gentleman sitting on a nearby bench. His face was wrinkled from the sun, his eyes a faded blue, but he smiled when we approached him.

I showed him the map and the name of the bakery.

He pointed to the map where it said *Ulica od Puca*.

We thanked him; he smiled, gathering every wrinkle in his face together and tipped his hat to us.

We passed many little shops. I knew Mario was waiting, but Ashley dragged me into each store, fascinated by the handmade lace and the even lacier gold pendants. The leather shop had a workroom where you could watcher the tradesmen sewing the leather for boots and purses. We also asked what the word "puc" meant. Seemed so many streets had the name. And we were told it meant 'wells.'

"Of course," I said to Ashely. "We've passed so many wells while strolling from shop to shop." I tugged at her arm, pointing to my watch. "We need to move quickly. Mario is waiting for me. You can shop on your way back and buy whatever you want."

Ashley sighed. "You never were a shopper. Fine. "She grinned at me. "I might even buy you a gift too."

"Fantastic. Now let's hurry."

Finally, after trudging up several blocks, we turned into an alley no wider than the two of us side by side, and there sat Mario, head in a newspaper, sipping coffee, dressed to perfection with his signature pullover sweater tied around his neck, a blue checked shirt, and jeans without a wrinkle.

Lining the wall was a narrow bench, a narrower table, and a chair.

I stood next to him. "Papa', we're here."

He looked at me, a smile lighting his bronzed face. "Olivia. Please sit."

He looked past me and froze, his eyes focused and unblinking, his mouth agape, his body taut.

I turned and looked at Ashley, the sun shining through her golden hair, giving her an angelic ethereal glow. Except for the shape of her face, she also looked exactly like our mother thirty-five years ago.

"I'm sorry, Mario. I should have warned you. This is my sister, Ashley."

He closed his mouth, but didn't smile.

Ashley reached to shake his hand. He took it, but couldn't speak. Staring at her for a moment, he finally dropped her hand. "This is a surprise." *Mio Dio. Angela is seeing this. What is she thinking? The face is the face of Veronica. The hair, the eyes. But her stature is tall and elegant, Veronica was petite. Angela, my love, stay calm.*

I leaned in to kiss him. "Are you okay, Papa'?"

"Yes, just surprised how much your sister looks like Veronica." He turned to Ashley. "I'm sorry, your name again?"

"It's Ashley. Maybe I should leave so you two can talk."

"No, no. Please sit. We need to prepare for Venice." He turned to me. "Your sister should have warned me, however."

A young man in black pants and white shirt appeared with two coffees and a piece of cake.

"This is the specialty. Carrot Cake. Best anywhere."

I could tell he was still flummoxed by Ashley's presence.

"Ashley has been very ill for the last twenty-four hours. She thought she caught a stomach virus on board. We were afraid Veronica would catch it. She's too fragile to be sick at this point. But it wasn't the virus." I was babbling out of sheer nervousness.

"I'm sorry, Ashley. I hope this isn't too sweet and heavy for your stomach."

"I love sweets. Thank you, I'll be fine." Ashley twisted her napkin and took a deep breath.

"So, Papa', we have told Mother you are here and when she will meet you. I've warned you, and Ashley will confirm Mother is not the woman you knew so many years ago. "

"And if you think you were thrown by seeing me," said Ashley, "You have no idea what to expect when seeing Veronica again."

He ignored her. "You read my letter, Olivia? Forgiveness? I still hear resentment and anger." Mario took my hand. "Can we give a dying woman peace?"

I put my arms around him and buried my face into his neck. "Of course, Mario. Of course we will do that." I could feel tears welling. I cleared my throat and forced a smile. "Let's enjoy the pastries and make our plans."

Mario lifted the cup to his lips, took a slow sip, and said, "First you tell her you found me, how you found me, give her the whole story. Tell her I've already forgiven her for keeping you from me. I think it best to meet in public first to give her some dignity, anonymity."

"How can you be anonymous in the middle of a crowd? Doesn't make sense to me," said Ashley.

"Ashley, Mom is like a piece of steel when presented with an audience. She'll want to appear dignified, but in private, she'll dissolve into a puddle of tears. You should know that by now."

"Fine." She gripped her cup and took a sip.

We talked for an hour about dinner in Venice and a place for Mario and Veronica to be alone, yet in public. He'd chosen a quiet restaurant facing the Rialto Bridge, right on the edge of the Grand Canal.

"When do I meet your family, your beautiful Angela, and the boys?" I turned to Ashley. "I met his daughter, Mia, in Taormina. We look a lot alike."

"Really," Ashley murmured.

I could tell she was tense. Mario excused himself, and went into the shop to pay. A woman with beautiful blond hair, tangled with wild curls, was sitting on a stool at the counter. I couldn't see her face, but I knew. I knew it was Mario's wife. There was a sense of intimacy between them, even though they never spoke. She'd been observing. And my stomach tightened. She was my biggest obstacle to having a relationship with my Father. And I prayed she'd forgiven him.

Mario came back with a bag of cookies for us. "Enjoy. You won't find cookies like this on the ship." He pulled me to him in a hug followed by the two-cheek kiss. "Everything is going to be good, Olivia. Everything." He stood back, his hands on my arms, and gazed into my eyes. "My family will love you."

He turned to Ashley. "I'm glad we met. You took me by surprise. But now I am ready for the contrast between young Veronica and how she is now."

"See you at the Rialto Bridge, Papa'," I whispered.

We turned and walked away, both of us relieved for very different reasons. I glanced back. Mario stood there watching. When we came to the end of the alley leading to the main street, I walked toward a statue and hid behind it for a few moments. I'd told Ashley to go to the right. I peeked around the statue. As I suspected, the blond woman was now wrapped in Mario's arms. I followed Ashley.

"The woman inside the bakery? It was Mario's wife. Still haven't seen her face except in photos, but she's forgiven him. I saw them together." I smiled and breathed a sigh of relief. "Would you mind going back to the ship by yourself? I promised I'd meet Tony this afternoon if I had time." I glanced at my watch. "I think I can still see him before we have to get back on the ship.

"Go for it. I like Tony. I've never seen you glow like you do when you're with him." She hugged me and wandered down the cobblestone path.

I knew she'd shop her way back to the ship.

I sent Tony a text giving him my location. I received his answer right away.

The café was difficult to find. I walked under the wall of the city and into Café Buza where the atmosphere was lacking but the view was stunning. Tony had his back to me and was sitting on a rickety chair, beer in hand, feet propped on a rail, soaking up the sun.

I walked quietly and planted a kiss on the back of his neck.

"I hope the woman who kissed me is Olivia. She's the only one who can give me chills."

I grabbed the seat next to him. He'd ordered the house white wine which arrived in a plastic cup with no apologies. The bar was devoid of any atmosphere. But the blue of the sea, the waves splashing against the rocks, and a handsome man beside me more than made up for the bohemian surroundings. On the rocks below people were sunbathing, some with clothes, and others naked.

We sat quietly, not needing to speak, holding hands. Tony sipped his beer, took off his sunglasses and turned to me. "Olivia, I'm aware we barely know each other. But I want you to know, I feel something with you so new to me that I find it almost frightening…yet solid." He pulled my lips to his, kissing me softly, without urgency. "Promise me you won't disappear after the cruise."

His eyes devoured me, drew me into his world. "I promise, Tony." I wanted him to kiss me again. But his annoying cell phone rang, interrupting our moment.

He glanced at the screen, pulled out some cash for the drinks, and stood up. "Come, my lovely lady. I'll escort you back to the ship."

Angela

Angela watched the women approach Mario. She recognized Olivia right away. But the other woman. Her stomach churned the moment she realized she was looking at the daughter of Veronica. She knew then how beautiful she must have been thirty-five years ago. How Mario had been tempted. Her hands curled into fists, her anger held tight within her.

Veronica is dying. She's not a threat to me. It was a long time ago. But damn him.

She watched until the meeting was over and waited until Olivia and her sister disappeared. She made her way to Mario. "Olivia is beautiful and looks just like our Mia. Hold me, Mario. Just hold me."

The Garden Suite
Oliva, Ashley, Veronica

Mother wrapped the blanket around her shoulders, her hands trembling. Her eyes darted between Ashley and me, glistened in tears. It was obvious she knew we wanted to "talk." And we knew she didn't want to hear us.

I'd ordered an early dinner sent up to the deck by our pool. The evening was balmy, a soft mist hovered over the deck, and music drifted from the sail-away party below.

Croatia dissolved into the distance, the dark clouds retreating, revealing a mass of lollipop-orange streaks in the sky. I read the exhaustion in my mother's eyes.

"This is nice," Veronica said, waving at the sky as it performed its end- of-day chromatography. "So why the private dinner, why the serious faces?" She squinted, holding her hand to shade her eyes.

Ashley offered her sunglasses. "Here, Mom. It's so bright right now."

Veronica placed the glasses over her ears but slid them down her nose as if to see us better. "What do you want? Is this an intervention? Am I going to die?" She chuckled. "Of course I'm doing to die...sooner than later." She smiled weakly. "But sooner?"

"Ashley and I want to discuss Venice and some plans before you go home."

"Go home to die, right? Have you already ordered hospice? Because I'm okay with that, really. And could I have a glass of wine?"

Ashley rolled her eyes and walked to the bar, poured a glass of her mother's favorite white zin, placed it on the table and sat next to her.

I had no idea how to start this conversation. I'd rehearsed it over and over in my mind, written notes, but there was no gentle way. I dove in. "Mom, tomorrow in Venice you will see a friend from a long time ago." I took her hand and leaned in close. "I know about my real father. I know Mario. I've met him, and he wants to see you tomorrow."

Her eyes widened. "What the..." She reached for her wine, took a sip, held her lips on the rim of the glass and swallowed. She gulped more and banged the glass on the table. Her eyes dropped to her now-folded hands on her lap.

"How do you know him?" She lifted her face to mine. "Once a few days ago when I was so tired and sick, I heard you mention his name. Did you, or was I dreaming?"

"I did, Mom. We thought you were dying from taking too many pills. I told you to hang on so you'd see Mario again."

Ashley knelt in front of Veronica. "Please tell us about him. It's okay; it's in the past and explains so many things."

"IT doesn't explain *anything*." Veronica's voice rose. "Mario was a result of the hell I lived with your father." She picked up the glass and drank the rest of the wine in one swallow. "You think you know everything. You don't. How dare you do this to me? Present me, a broken, sickly old woman to the man I loved more than life itself? To show him what I've become. How dare you strip me of whatever pride I have left?"

She threw the wineglass across the deck. Shards skittered across the deck.

Ashley jumped. I glared.

Her eyes swept me up and down. "I didn't know who your father was until three months after you were born. The hair, the eyes…left no doubt. I was sleeping with Mario, loving him. At the same time, your father's so-called lovemaking was like rape night after night. Or, he was too drunk to perform and blamed me. It was a no-win for me." She flung the blanket from her shoulders, strode across the patio with a strength she didn't have, rattled through the glasses and poured more wine. "And don't think he wouldn't have hit you and taken his frustration out on you. I protected both of you." She leaned on the table, exhausted. She turned and staggered to her chair, sat down, and threw the blanket over her shoulders, her face twisted, tears flowing, lips pursed, and stared at us as though she'd retreated into another world.

Ashley stood and looked at me, eyes so wide I thought they'd locked into place. I stood next to her, placing my arm around her waist and whispered, "It's okay, Ash. We have to do this." I tugged at her waist, and then reached for her shoulders, shaking her. She blinked.

"Don't dump your guilt on us, Mom," I pleaded. "The past is past. My childhood from age twelve was miserable. I lived in fear of an angry father and a drunk mother. I had no friends come to my house. My happiness took place at the homes of normal friends. So leave it alone."

I paced across the patio. The sun hung low now, blood red. I crossed the deck to switch on the lights. I felt like the air had evaporated. I walked toward my mother, sat down next to her, and took her hand.

"Just tell me about Mario. Why didn't you tell me the truth?"

"Why would I?"

"Because I deserved to know." I took a cleansing breath and repeated softly, "Because I deserved to know." I watched the sky darken.

"Here's the thing, Mom. I've met Mario, here in Italy. He remembers you as a beautiful, enchanting, fun-loving and passionate woman. When he describes you, he's talking about someone I've never known."

Veronica glared, looking straight ahead. "Which is why I don't want to see him, ever!" She turned. "Don't you understand? He made me feel different, alive, happy, loved."

"You need to ask his forgiveness for keeping me a secret. He needs to have your forgiveness for making a baby with you. It was thirty-five years ago. We all need completion. Please?"

"Get me some more wine, Ashley."

"But Mother…"

"Don't boss me. Happiest day of my life was when you moved out and got married and took that burden away from me."

Ashley stiffened.

I got as close to my mother's face as I could. "Do not speak to Ashley like that, or to me. You are going to meet Mario and his family tomorrow. And you will beg his forgiveness for keeping me, his first-born-child, a secret. Make it right."

I padded away from her to the railing of the ship and peered down, the light of the day gone. My heart and soul felt as dark as the sea. I hated my Mother at that moment, and I knew it would do me no good to continue this conversation. My life was going to change. Veronica was, is, my mother. I'll take care of her. But I don't have to be her buddy. I pounded the railing and turned.

"Ashley, let's go to the martini bar." I grabbed a startled Ashley by the arm and towed her to the elevator.

"Mom, we arrive in Venice tomorrow. Make up your mind. Meet Mario and make it right or sit in a hotel room and wait for your flight home. I'm done begging."

A loud ding announced the arrival of the lift. We walked in, and turned to the closing doors. Veronica sat in the same position, still, expressionless.

At that moment, I didn't care!

I burst into the glowing martini bar with enough heat and anger to melt the ice counter. Ashley followed me.

"Calm down, Olivia. She'll go with us tomorrow."

"Don't care right now, Ash." I craned my neck to search for Tony. He'd probably given up on me.

Ashley grabbed my arm and held firm. "She'll forget all about our little tiff. I'll fix her up so she doesn't look like a bag lady."

"Help me find Tony," I said.

"You know full well how good I am with makeup and hair."

I turned to face her. "Look, dear Sis, Mom looks like someone who has one foot in the grave and the other on the proverbial banana peel. Nothing is going to 'fix her up'."

Ashley laughed. "Good thing Tony can't see your face now." She put her hands on her hips. "Fact is, Mom does have one foot in the grave. But I guarantee she will look presentable tomorrow. And she'll just 'happen' to meet with Mario, and it will be fine. Trust me."

"What's wrong?" Tony walked up behind me and slid his arm around my shoulder.

I breathed in his scent, the manly cologne that always lingered on my clothing long after we'd been together. I turned and gazed into his espresso eyes and felt my body relax.

"Hey, Tony. Nothing's wrong, really. I'm fine." I smiled, hoping my anger wasn't obvious.

Ashley laughed. "One minute earlier and you'd have had the privilege of seeing her angry face. It wasn't pretty."

"What's the matter?" he asked, tucking his finger under my chin.

I shivered. "It's my mom. She was giving us a hard time, and I reacted badly." I turned to glare at Ash.

"Come on, gals," Tony said. "Let's find a place in the corner where we can talk. I'll order up your favorite martinis. Dirty Girl Scout, right?" He placed himself between us, took our hands, and walked us to a hidden and dim section of the 'Glacier Bar.'

"Sit quietly, no arguing, no chatting about Mom, breathe deep, and I'll fetch the drinks. "He started to walk away, turned, pointed his finger at us, and said, "I mean it. Stay silent." With a grin, he strode toward the bar.

"He's a gem, Olivia. A keeper. Don't blow it."

"You never were one for obeying orders, were you? Tony said to be silent. I refuse to discuss anything until he comes back." I picked up the martini menu and read every word, trying to hold my tongue.

"Honestly, Olivia. Let some of that passionate Italian blood that flows through your veins shine. Lighten up."

"S I L E N C E!" I closed my eyes, wanting to shut out the scene with my mother. But I kept hearing her cruel words.

"Okay. I'll just sit here quietly until Tony returns. But when he comes back, we are all going to talk. Maybe he can help you calm down about tomorrow."

I glared at her. "Dog with bone!"

"Okay, I see neither of you followed my orders." Tony smiled, right dimple prominent. The waiter walked behind him with the drink tray. Tony settled into the chair between us while the martinis were placed onto the table.

"Now, Olivia, we need to make plans for Venice after your sister and mom leave." He turned to Ashley. "I'll take care of your sister's attitude. Not to worry." He patted her hand.

"Thanks, Tony." She leaned over to kiss him on the cheek. "Now let's hash things out."

With a deep breath, she began. "Olivia has a right to be angry with Mom. But I promised her I would fix Mom up to look, if not like she did 35 years ago, at least really good for her age and condition. Now Olivia," she glanced at me, "has a perfectly legitimate reason to doubt me. But by tomorrow, Mom will have forgotten our spat, and I know I can make it a good meeting."

Tony turned to me. "Olivia, don't you think Ashley deserves to try? It will make tomorrow so much easier on everyone." He placed his hands on my face and leaned in for a kiss, taking my breath away.

"Fine."

"Hey, Ash, she said 'fine.'"

Tony lifted his glass. "A toast to the two prettiest women on the ship. *Cin Cin.*"

I drank my martini as if it were a glass of water and felt the warmth of the alcohol immediately. "Hmmmm. This is delicious, although a bit strong."

"I paid extra to double the vodka, the Kahlua, the Bailey's Irish cream, and tripled the white crème de men-the. Enjoy!" Tony grinned.

"Bottoms up, Ashley," I said to my sister. "Drink and get out of here so Tony and I can talk."

Ashley, who usually sips a drink, gulped it down. "Goodnight, young lovers." She rose and floated away.

"Now, we've taken care of all temporary problems. Let's talk about us, Olivia." Tony kissed me again, and the room spun.

I took a deep breath. "Okay, let's start with your secrets."

"No, let's start with yours. From what I can see, the real Olivia has been under cover this whole cruise. I've seen her a few times." He leaned in for another kiss. "But when we have alone time in Venice, I hope you're relaxed enough to trust me."

Tony pulled my head onto his shoulder and rubbed my arm gently. "I'm crazy about you. I'm starting a whole new life in another month. I'd like to see if you can be a part of it."

"I'd like that, Tony." I wrapped my free arm around him and snuggled in close. I could hear the beating of his heart. "But I need to know three things. Who the heck is the 'Putin-like-man' named, Joe; who's the obnoxious tourist you've been watching; and are you CIA?"

"What?" Tony broke away, looking at me. "No. No I am not CIA. But I do work for a firm that does undercover work for the government. I've given my notice. I need to make a big change in my life. And how did you figure any of this out?"

I laughed. "Let's just say, I'm very cautious about men. I haven't missed much. You can tell me everything in Venice. Kiss me again, Tony."

"Let's get out of here."

He took me by the hand and led me out onto the open deck. We leaned against the railing and watched the shimmering stars, breathing in the fresh ocean air. I noticed another cruise ship in the distance, its lights sparkling in the blackness of the night.

"When and where will we meet?"

Tony pulled me close. "We'll meet on the Piazza San Marcos at noon on Sunday in front of the cabana with the jazz trio. Just look for the piano. I'll be there."

He lifted my face to his. "All I want to do now is kiss you and convince you to keep that date, no matter what."

The kiss seemed to last for hours, and I was lost in its promise and sensuality. When Tony finally pulled away, I said in a ragged voice, "There's no way I'll miss that date, Tony." I pulled him in for one last kiss. "I'll see you at disembarkation tomorrow morning and at the Piazza on Sunday."

I arrived at my room, not remembering how I got there, never seeing another passenger, and not hearing any music or chatter. When I closed the door to my room, I leaned against it and sighed, tears falling. *Maybe, just maybe, I'm going to at last have two men in my life I can trust and who will love me unconditionally.*

My stomach tightened, the pain intense. There lingered, with a bit of fear, a dread of meeting my father's family. And, with pleasurable excitement, the happiness of seeing Tony in Venice.

Day Twelve
Venice, Italy
Disembarkation Day

The alarm awakened me at once. After a long stretch of arms and legs, I let my thoughts wander to last night and Tony's promise to meet me in Venice. My heart warmed, thankful my sister and I were now on the same side. And Mother…well, today would finish that story, her story of Mario at least.

I walked to the curtains and flung them back. There was a smudge of orange hanging over the early-morning fog. The heavy mist shrouded the church spires and domes, ethereal features peeking through the mist. Flecks of gold glimmered while the ship navigated the narrow entrance to

Venice. Even with a semi-blocked view, the city was awe-inspiring. The fish-shaped island seemed to undulate with mystery as she revealed herself with each change of light.

My heart pumped with excitement, reminding me I had an appointment with my true roots…a family in Venice.

A knock on the door punctured my happiness.

"Olivia, I need help getting Mother ready." Ashley pounded the door again. "Did you hear me?"

With a sigh, I strolled to the door, opened it, and once again was taken by my sister's beauty. This was how our mother must have looked when she met Mario. It had always surprised me when Ashley entered a room. Whenever she entered, the room filled with her presence. Mom must have been the same way in her younger years. Or was it her father Ashley portrayed? Maybe Mom had been shy. It was too late for me to discover the real Veronica. But Mario had seen something wonderful. And I would try to see her through his eyes.

"Why are you staring at me?" Ashley asked. "Come on. Christopher is here to help with the luggage, and Mom is already complaining about of having to be awakened 'in the middle of the damn night.'"

"I'm coming. Give me a minute to shut the suitcase I'm sending home with you."

Sadness squeezed me as I shoved one last pair of shoes into the luggage, closed and locked it, and fastened my colored tag for a ten o'clock departure from the ship. Closing the suitcase reminded me how everything had changed in the last ten days. I hated to see my sister leave tomorrow, and hoped our relationship would continue to move forward with love and understanding, and most of all, enjoyment of each other's company.

The possibility my Mother would die before I returned to California pressed heavily on me. I rolled my shoulders to try to shrug off the feeling. I had to stay in Venice for awhile. I practiced my deep breathing…in and hold…out…blowing away the guilt. It was Mario's turn to be a part of my life. Yet, despite all her faults, I loved my mother.

I was more than grateful for Christopher's help packing last night and even more thrilled I didn't have to lug this over-sized baggage to my hotel. Ashley had offered to put it on the plane with her even though it would cost her an extra hundred dollars.

I grabbed my cup of coffee from the top of the bureau and walked next door to Ashley's room. Whether Mom knew it or not, it looked like she was ready to meet Mario.

Ashley had settled our Mom into the chair in front of the vanity and was working furiously on her thin and straggly hair. Ashley waved me in and motioned for me to sit next to Mom as she pulled and yanked on Mom's hair, working the round brush and hair dryer at the same time. My eyes widened watching her magically transform the hair into a shiny do.

Ash set the dryer down. "Well, what do you think?"

"You're a miracle worker. Mom, do you like your hair?"

She grinned. "It's lovely," she answered softly.

"Don't cry," said Ashley. "You cannot cry. I just did your foundation. Dab at your eye with a tissue if you must, but do NOT cry. Please."

Ashley worked more magic on Mom, moisturizing, blending makeup, thickening her sparse eyelashes, adding a pink blush to her cheeks and soft golden beige to her eyes. She used a light hand, but as she added color, Mom's eyes brightened to their former blue. She looked frail but lovely considering her circumstances.

"Wow, Ash, you should do this for a living."

"Yeah, right." She stood behind Mom and put her hands on her shoulders. "How do you feel now? And don't you dare get all weepy on me."

Veronica reached back and patted Ashley's hand. "You're a wonderful daughter. I think I look like I might not die right away." She touched her hair, then her cheek.

"One final touch." Ashley took a pink lip gloss and applied it to Veronica's lips. "There you go. Now let's get you dressed."

Ashley walked to the closet and pulled out a pair of beige linen pants and a Robin's egg blue short sleeved sweater.

I helped Ashley get her dressed. Whether mom knew it or not, she was ready to meet Mario. I'd arranged the meeting last night with him. They would just 'happen' to see each other.

"Come on, gals. Christopher has arranged a simple breakfast for us before we disembark." Ashley started to walk toward the large open patio on top of the ship.

"Wait," Veronica called. "It's cold out there."

"The ship is barely moving, there's no breeze, and the sun is starting to shine. This way, we can watch Venice unfold before we dock. Now come on." Ashley strode to the table where Christopher waited.

Christopher pushed in our chairs, draped napkins over our laps and began to serve us coffee and juice, set the rolls and fruit on the table, and excused himself to gather our luggage.

"Just a moment, Christopher," said Ashley. "I have something for you." She placed an envelope in his pocket. She'd been handing envelopes to everyone who'd given us such great service throughout the cruise.

Christopher bowed. "Thank you. I hope you ladies have a wonderful time in Venice and a safe flight home."

"And I will definitely request you on my next cruise," said Ashley, smiling broadly.

"I'm happy to say you won't see me again," said Christopher. "I'm going home tomorrow to start a new life and a new career. This isn't the career for me."

"Best of luck to you," I said, shaking his hand. "Never had a butler before, but you managed to make it a dream cruise beyond my expectations." I smiled warmly.

"However, Christopher, I have one question for you," I said, looking at him with narrowed eyes. "I need to know if you and Tony are more than just butler and passenger. You work for the same company, don't you? "

He dropped my hand. "What?"

I chuckled. "Being raised in a home with alcohol and verbal abuse gives one an edge in life. Did you know that? You're always looking for signs. You read facial and body language so you are prepared when 'something bad' happens. The body language between you and Tony screamed at times about both of you being involved in some sort of relationship outside the confines of this ship."

"Then I guess it's a good thing we're both changing professions, isn't it?"

"That's it? No more information?"

"Nope. If you think you have extra-sensory radar with people, then you can figure it out, right?"

With a droll grin, he pulled out his cell and called for two more stewards to help with the luggage and stood by the elevator. While pulling the suitcases into the elevator, he smiled. "I've noticed a lot of people are undercover on this ship, including you." With a salute, he disappeared behind the closing doors.

I stood still, contemplating what he'd just said. Was I undercover? Hmmmm. I guess for the first part of the cruise I was carrying a huge secret, certainly keeping my father's existence under my hat, so to speak. I took another deep breath.

"Let's eat," I said. "I'm starved. And we have a lot of walking to do today." I placed my linen napkin on my lap and took a huge bite of my croissant, lost in thoughts of Venice. I felt a tightening in my stomach, wondering and worrying how Mario's family would accept me.

The disembarkation process was easy. Christopher escorted us to a private lounge next to the concierge office. He took us to a table with a "reserved" sign on it.

"This is where we officially say goodbye," said Christopher. "I'll send the hostess to you with coffee and pastries while you wait for your van. It's been a pleasure to serve you."

"Thanks for everything," I said.

Once our coffee and rolls arrived, we watched while three workers from the ship loaded our luggage into the large blue van. An ornate emblem emblazoned the side of the van. *Luna Baglioni, Venezia.* My sister had obviously booked a five-star hotel. Worked for me.

A young man in the lounge approached us. "Your van has arrived. Please follow me."

The entire disembarkation process had taken less than an hour.

A well-dressed man with bronzed skin and impossibly thick silver hair stood next to the van holding a sign with our names printed in black blocked letters.

"Buon giorgno, " said Ashley, handing him an enveloped I assumed contained our reservation.

"Prego," he said, helping Ashley into the back seat. He turned to me and offered his hand, helping me into the van next to Ashley.

The driver then pulled out a set of steps and gently assisted Mother into the front seat.

She smiled at such special treatment. And I marveled at how good she looked. And felt immense relief she was so calm.

The ride was short, and we stopped at a canal where two speed boats awaited us. Gleaming and polished wood on the exterior of the boats had me wondering if they'd ever been in water. One pilot took our luggage and the other pilot assisted us into the smaller vessel to take us to our hotel.

The Grand Canal was full of boats from small taxis to barges and many *vaporettos*, the Venice version of a bus on water. The mansions on the waterfront were colorful. We were going so fast, it was difficult to study the elegant fifteenth century architecture. The water was not clear and had a musty smell which worsened as we navigated the narrower canals. In less than ten minutes, we arrived at the entrance of the hotel. The dock was surrounded by bright red and yellow striped poles and steps leading up to the lobby. Electric red geraniums burst from yellow ceramic pots lining the sidewalk. We walked into a lobby of glass walls, ceilings filled with white flowered Venetian glass chandeliers. It took my breath away. Conversation stopped. Even my mother, for once, was speechless. She gazed at everything, mouth unattractively open.

A tall lady dressed in a cream-colored suit, a strand of pearls adorning her neck greeted us in accented English. "Good morning. Mrs. Morgan-Brown?"

Ashley took the lady's extended hand. "Yes. I texted you from the taxi."

"I'm Chiara D'Angelo. You've been checked in. I'll show you to your rooms."

We followed her, appreciating her slow pace. It was obvious she had taken note of my mother's condition.

When we arrived at my room, our hostess opened the door.

I walked into a room of gold and coral. A draped canopy hung over my bed. The Venetian glass chandeliers sparkled with yellow and coral flowers. The doors to the terrace opened onto a view of a lagoon the color of peacocks in the sunrise.

"Get settled, Olivia," said Ashley, "since you'll be here for a few days. Mom and I will only need our overnight case to unpack. Our plane leaves at ten tomorrow morning. Enjoy your room." She smiled and took mom's arm and followed the hostess to their suite.

I plopped into one of the luscious upholstered chairs and couldn't believe my eyes. A five-star luxury hotel had never been within my budget, even when married to the old ex- husband. He preferred to spend money on parties and…I didn't want to go there.

I envisioned Tony here with me. My body tingled at the thought. But I needed to be with Tony in the real world and get to know him better. The physical attraction was there, sizzling like a live electrical line every time we were together. But my trust in men needed some upgrading before I plunged into a relationship or short-term affair of the heart.

Shake it off, Olivia. Shake it off!

I began to unpack what I needed for the next few days. I'd be back to Venice soon. But this time, now, would make or break my future with my father. If the family didn't accept me, my relationship would be with him alone. And I wanted more.

I heard my phone ding with a text.

"Bring everyone, 1 p.m., to Ristorante Terrzaa Sommariva. Download map. Veronica will need to rest. You will see me on the Rialto Bridge. Papa'

Tears filled my eyes. It was the first time he hadn't used his name, Mario. I walked to the patio, and gazed at the lagoon. It was almost time to meet the family. The smooth-as-glass water seemed like a sign…that the day would be as smooth. Veronica would see Mario, and hopefully this circle of life and lies would be resolved. I prayed it would be so.

Primping for a special occasion is an Olympic sport for women. And the time and effort the three of us put into getting ready for our lunch would have won us a gold medal.

Ashley appeared ageless and stunning in her pale daisy-yellow capris and creamy sleeveless tank top. She seemed to have an extra air of confidence today. Her golden hair swept straight back from her face, accentuating her classic Nordic features. Her cerulean blue eyes were wide and filled with hope.

Mother, transformed by Ashley, looked alive, though thin.

But I struggled. I had to impress a family who might not accept me. I knew what I was on the inside trumped my appearance. But first impressions count with most people.

"Help me, Sis. I can't decide what to wear." I stood helplessly in front of the floor- to- ceiling gilded mirror, holding two dresses; one, cobalt blue, the other a black sundress with a halter top.

"Wear the black." Ashley stood behind me and grabbed the blue dress, tossing it onto a nearby chair. "This shows off your figure, yet it's still modest. And I want to fix your hair to emphasize your curls, get it off your face. Then," she said, waving a makeup brush in the air, "I am going to make those eyes pop and add more bronze highlights to your face."

I smiled. *Ashley in control? How'd that happen? And why was I okay with this…feeling happy and comforted?*

She almost shoved me into the chair in front of the vanity. Peering over my shoulder, she played with my hair for awhile. "Hmmmm? Hmmm?" She grinned and said, "Got it. You are going to look more Italian than the Italians, and there will be no doubt you belong to Mario! No doubt at all." And with the flourish of a symphonic conductor, she played with my hair, brushing, spraying, crunching, pulling, until my hair looked like a model's on an Italian billboard. She tossed the hairbrush onto the bed behind her and started on my face, scrubbing it raw with some of her sand-filled cream.

"Ouch. Don't be so rough, Ash."

"I'm just sloughing the dead skin off so you glow. Trust me," she said, massaging my cheeks. She gathered her tools, laying them on the counter in an orderly line and began to work her magic. When she finished, she placed her hands on my shoulder and leaned her head next to mine.

"You are truly a beautiful woman, Olivia." Smiling broadly, she whispered, "I love you. I really do love you, Sis."

I felt the tears pool.

"No! No! Stop! I'm sorry. This isn't the time for sentiment.."

She grabbed a tissue, ready to repair any damage a falling tear might cause and went to fetch my dress.

Ten minutes later, black sundress accented by black and white chandelier earrings and sling back black sandals, I felt like a new woman. It was me, but classier, thanks to my sister. And I had to admit I felt more confident.

We gathered my mom and our purses and stood in line for a water taxi. The polished mahogany boats bobbled in the water, ready for the line of customers. Number thirty-four approached the dock and the pilot helped us bundle mom into the taxi and took off to the Rialto Bridge. We sat in comfort on the soft-leather-upholstered-bench seats. I wanted to stand up in the back and let the wind rip through my hair.

"Sit down," Ashley commanded. "You're hair will be a mess."

I sat.

Mom's cheeks were so rosy, it was difficult to imagine she had such a short time left here with us. I pushed that thought aside, realizing how much I wished we had more time to make things right.

The water was rough at the dock near the Rialto Bridge. It was a struggle to assist mom from the boat onto the dock.

We crept along at mom's pace, not wanting to exhaust her. I didn't even notice the beauty of Venice. None of us wanted to fall, or trip on the slippery cobblestone sidewalks, still wet from the soft morning rain. We turned a corner into a narrow walkway leading to the restaurant right on the canal. I looked toward the bridge and saw Mario walk toward us. He sat at an umbrella table. His mop of glorious white hair glowed. His crisp dark blue shirt enhanced his bronzed skin. He smiled. I smiled. We continued to walk towards him.

I noticed his eyes widen at seeing Ashley, a slight intake of breath followed by an uncertain smile upon seeing Veronica. He stood and waited.

Ashley held Mom's arm while I walked to Mario and kissed him on the cheek. "Thank you, my daughter. Thank you for this moment." He walked toward Veronica as though in slow motion and took her hand.

"Veronica. After all these years." He sighed then cupped her face with his hands. "Nica."

Mother stood still as a wooden soldier. Tears puddled then fell.

"Rio?"

He guided her with a gentle hand to a seat and sat next to her, his eyes never wavering from hers. "It's been a long time."

Dear God. What happened to her? The light no longer shines in her blue eyes. Her posture is defeated and weak. This can't be Veronica.

"Mother, Olivia and I are going to start walking to the restaurant. We'll see you in a few minutes. Are you okay?"

She did not answer. She could only stare. She folded her hands and looked down.

We left them. Alone, at the table and made our way to meet the family gathered on the bridge above us.

"Please don't cry Nica." He stroked her cheek and brushed a stray hair from her forehead. He pressed his thumb under her eyes to wipe away tears.

"Don't cry?" Her voice was barely audible, eyes once again downcast. "I've been crying for you for thirty-five years, every time I looked at our daughter." She hung her head.

"It's okay, Nica. It's okay."

The world stopped for them. Memories took the place of words, transporting them to a lifetime ago in Los Angeles when they were young and happy, in love.

"I'm sorry I've ruined so many lives." She trembled, burying her face in her hands.

Silence.

Footsteps echoed off the granite buildings, heels clicked while people rushed to appointments. In the corner, in front of a clothing store, a young couple argued … perhaps a lovers' spat.

In the distance, an espresso machine wooshed, the sound of steam rushing through the grounds, creating a creamy dark coffee.

Mario glanced at the waiter standing by for an order and shook his head. The waiter left, shrugging his shoulders. Mario's stomach rumbled with hunger. The aroma of simmering sauce filled his nostrils. He sighed, remembering.

Where was the beauty of long ago? Angela still carried her beauty inside and out. Nico's disease-ridden body was frail beyond his comprehension. But it was the brightness and laughter she always carried in her eyes that had vanished, as though someone had erased her very core.

He looked at the couple, their hands waving. It reminded him of the fights with Angela over the years. But he loved that fire in her. Veronica used to have so much passion and energy.

"What happened, Veronica?"

"What happened? You left to marry your sweetheart."
It was a whisper, barely audible over the clatter surrounding them.

"Look at me, Nica."

She turned her head away, staring at nothing, seeing nothing. "Would you have come back?"

"We said goodbye. You said goodbye to me."

Silence.

Tears continued down Veronica's cheeks.

Mario handed her his freshly ironed handkerchief.

"We both agreed it was over. Even though we loved each other, we agreed. But I would have done the right thing if I'd known a baby was involved."

"You'd have married me?" She twisted her hair, but looked down.

"No, but I would have been a part of Olivia's life. I'd never abandon a child."

She turned, her countenance twisted in anger. "My husband would never have allowed it. He hated me when he realized she was not his child."

One of the many immigrants hawking flowers walked by, stopped, and offered a rose to Mario.

"No, *grazie.*"

"Lady sad. Flower?"

With a sigh of impatience, Mario pulled out his wallet and offered one euro to the man, took the flower, and set it on the table.

Veronica squeezed her eyes shut, remembering the last night with Mario. He'd held her, gazing at her with his large gray eyes, stroking her body. She knew she'd never see him again. She'd felt a flutter in her stomach, knowing she was carrying a child. But whose child? She didn't know. And she'd let him go.

"Nico? What are you thinking?"

"Of our last night together."

Silence.

"Why did you take advantage of me?" She looked at him, her makeup now caked with dried tears.

"Veronica, we both knew we were wrong. I don't remember any regrets at the time by me. Nor do I remember you protesting. I didn't know you were married at first. Look at me. I didn't know. You told me after our first night together."

"I need an espresso," she said.

Mario waved the waiter to the table and ordered.

Veronica remained silent until the coffee arrived. She took a sip. "You never told me about your fiancé."

"Accusations will get us nowhere, Nica. Nowhere. We fell in love. We created a child. And Olivia came from the love we had. It was real."

He sipped his coffee, placed the cup back onto the table, and picked up the rose. "Here, Nica. I offer this to you and ask for your forgiveness. I was wrong to love you. Will you forgive me?"

He regretted his tone of voice.

She looked at him, blinking back tears. "Dear Rio, I've always loved you. You gave me two gifts. Your love and Olivia. I made all the wrong choices. I drank. I became a terrible mother."

She stopped speaking and placed her blue-veined, shaking hand on his cheek. "I could have held my head high and put every ounce of my life into those girls. I could have stood up to my abusive husband." She drew in a ragged breath. "But I didn't. I chose to bury myself in alcohol and deserved my miserable life."

Hanging her head, her hands folded tightly together, she whispered, "Please forgive me. Forgive me for denying you a daughter, for not being a good mother, for everything. I thought you could save me from my miserable life."

She looked into his eyes. "Forgive me."

Mario pulled her head onto his shoulder. And they wept quietly, washing away a lifetime of regrets while the piazza continued its buzz of people going about their lives.

Mario whispered, "My wife would like to meet you." He paused, feeling her body tense. "She wants to be a part of Olivia's life after…" He stopped.

"After I die?" She breathed in, then exhaled slowly. "I'd like that, Rio. To know Olivia will have a family."

Mario stood and offered her his hand. She took his arm instead, her other hand clutching the rose.

"No regrets, Veronica."

"None, Mario."

They walked slowly, Mario guiding the fragile Veronica.

The pewter skies spit out a mist, but when she saw Olivia waiting for them, Mario noticed a hint of bright blue in her eyes.

"She seems happier now, doesn't she Rio? Our Olivia?"

"Si, Nica. Olivia e' felice e contenta." He patted her hand.

They walked across the alley into the tiny square where Ashley and Olivia waited. Olivia's eyes brimmed with tears, but her smile was an arrow of sunshine piercing the gray sky.

"She has your eyes, Mario."

"And Ashley has yours." He sighed.

Olivia

I smiled, tears ready to overflow at the sight of my frail mother and my strong father, arm in arm, at peace.

"Look at them, Olivia," said Ashley, grabbing my hand. "Mom looks younger. And there's a glimmer in those old blue eyes."

"Yup. I think it's going to be okay." Ashley handed me a tissue, always concerned about makeup being ruined. "Let's go meet them."

Mario held onto Veronica's hand and hugged Olivia with his free arm. He kissed Ashley on the cheek and whispered, *"Sei bellissima!"*

Ashley put her arm around her mother's waist. "We need to get to our hotel, Mom. We can say goodbye here."

Mario hung his head, quiet, leaving an awkward silence. He reached for his cell phone.

"*Ciao, cara mia.*" He walked away, speaking in a whisper.

I looked at Ashley, shrugging my shoulders. "I have no idea who he's calling."

"I know," Veronica said. "He's asking permission to bring me to his home. And I don't think I can do it." She turned to Ashley. "Just take me back to the hotel. We have to leave so early in the morning. I'm tired."

I screamed inside, watching the light leave my mother's eyes.

Mario strode back to us, his hand waving wildly, yelling, "We're all going to my house. Come."

"But I'm not well, and your wife?" Veronica protested, sputtering.

"*Va bene, Rica.* It's fine. Angela wants to meet you. You'll love my family."

"Just for a bit, Mother," Olivia said, taking Veronica's hand. "You can see my Italian family and know I will be okay."

Veronica whispered, "I'm afraid."

"*Non c'e problema,* Veronica. Just for an hour. Come. My boat is waiting on the canal around the corner."

I smiled at my father, but inside I wondered if this was such a good idea for my mother.

It seemed strange to be here, in my father's home with my new-found family. The living room, filled with my siblings, was loud with laughter and everyone talking over each other; sauces simmered in the kitchen, rich aromas swirling in the air. I watched Angela cooking with Mia and yearned to join them.

But on the balcony, with the sliding doors closed, sat Veronica, my mother, leaning on the table, chatting with my father. Seeing the two of them together caused an explosion of emotion inside me. Mario's face widened into a smile, and Mom actually smiled back at him, her frail hand resting on his arm as he spoke. Angela had welcomed her warmly and had set the patio table with coffee, water and a tray of antipasti. She'd been the one to quietly close the doors to give them privacy.

I couldn't erase Mario's expression of shock when he first saw Veronica. He'd covered it beautifully, pausing slightly before he kissed her on the cheek. And moments ago, Angela greeted her with a kiss, as did my two brothers and my sister, Mia. Mario had told me Angela had forgiven him and the family had accepted the situation.

The moment I'd told Veronica about finding my father, she'd seemed to brighten and gain a bit of strength. I took a sip of wine, swirling the dark *Brunello chianti,* remembering our conversation.

"You know Mario?" Mother's voice was strong. "How, when, oh dear. Such a terrible secret I've kept from you. But how?"

I had pulled her closer to me, hugging her. "It doesn't matter how. What matters is you and Mario will see each other again." I kissed her cheek and brushed away the strings of gray hair falling on her forehead. "Are you happy?"

"I don't want him to see me like this, Olivia." She turned to my sister. "Ashley, please. I want him to remember me like I used to be."

"It's okay. He knows you're very ill."

"Not just that. I kept something from him. It was so wrong. He'll hate me. Hate me. He'll hate me." Her eyes had clouded with fear.

Ashley had knelt in front of her. "No, Mom. He's a wonderful, forgiving man. His family knows everything. They all want to meet you."

She shook her head, covered her face with her hands, and wept. "I loved him. I did. But I had to protect everyone, Ashley, everyone."

"Mom, remember our talk yesterday. About forgiveness, and moving on with our lives? It's okay. You and Mario need to see each other, to remember, to share your daughter with each other. Please, Mom?"

But Veronica had exhausted herself with emotion and leaned her head on my shoulder and closed her eyes.

"Are we doing the right thing, Ash? Will she survive this?"

"We're all going to be fine. She'll sleep well tonight and tomorrow we'll meet Mario as planned. Let's get her to bed." Ashley lifted Mother and carried her like a baby to her bed.

I'd sat there, wondering if I could handle seeing my parents together for the first time.

I felt a tap on my shoulder and jumped. I looked up at Angela.

"I'm sorry, Angela. I was daydreaming."

"I understand. I think we've all been doing a bit of daydreaming over the last few days." She smiled at me. "Olivia? Would you like to join us in the kitchen? I think you're worrying about my Mario and Veronica. *Non paura.* Come. You need to know how to make my sauce if you're going to be a part of this family."

I glanced toward the patio. "Sure. I want to learn. But I have to warn you, I'm a novice in the kitchen. Mom's kitchen skills were non-existent. I never learned much."

"Come. I teach you." Angela took my arm, led me into the aroma-filled space and threw an apron at me. "Put it on. You don't want to spill sauce all over you."

I donned the apron and began to stir, the pleasant aromas filling me with a sense of home and happiness. Mia hummed as she stood beside me shredding lettuce for the salad.

"You know, my mama was *molto gelosa,*" Mia whispered.

"What? I speak little Italian. Did you say jealous?"

"Si. Anch'io." She put the lettuce down and leaned in closer. "It was difficult, fighting, many uh *pioggia.*" She drew tears with her fingers.

"Ah, tears, crying. *Capisco.*" I rested my hand on her arm. "But now?"

"Now is okay." Mia smiled. "I think I like a sister. My brothers…sons are always better with Italian family, *capice*?"

"Si, capisco." I gave her a hug, remembering our one and only meeting in Taormina. She'd been hostile. Not that I could blame her. But our time had not been pleasant.

"Stir, Olivia," demanded Angela. "No stop."

Mia rolled her eyes. "Very bossy. She likes you."

I pulled the spoon to my mouth, blew gently and tasted the sauce. The texture was smooth, yet crunchy with the pine nuts, and salty with the flavors of the olive oil, garlic, the basil turning the sauce a beautiful shade of green and coating the hot pasta to perfection.

I glanced toward the patio, trying to get Ashley's attention. I could tell from Mom's slumped shoulders she was tired. As if reading my mind, Mario stood and helped her inside.

To everyone's surprise, Angela ran over to her and led Veronica into a bedroom, yelling something over her shoulder. I assumed she'd said she needed to lie down.

Mario stood open-mouthed. Soon a smile lit up his face. His Angela was a good woman, a forgiving woman. *She's accepted my daughter.* He drew in a deep breath, sighed, and strolled into the kitchen. His smile deepened watching Olivia and Mia working together on the family dinner.

The family dinner around the grand mahogany table proved boisterous, loud, and chaotic, everyone talking at once. Veronica slept through it all. Mario sat at the head of the table watching every movement, listening to all conversations, speaking little, face lit into a permanent smile.

I slid my hand under the table and rested it on his knee. He placed his hand on mine, patting it gently. My stomach relaxed, my heart beat with happiness, and I knew I'd found home. It might have taken longer than most people for it to happen. But as I sat there, my hand covered by the warmth of my papa's strong hand, I knew my future would hold more happiness than sorrow.

St. Mark's Square simmered with tourists and pigeons. Gathering clouds threatened an oncoming storm. I didn't care. I sipped my espresso and stared at nothing in particular. Yesterday's events had been the worst of my entire life, even more painful than being dumped by a cheating husband. But the afternoon–a reunion, forgiveness, a new family.

My mother and Ashley had boarded their plane for California less than three hours ago. I prayed mom would survive until I returned to California. My emotions remained on the numb side. But part of me felt free and happy. My family had been restored to me. I'd found a new relationship with my sister, a mom who loves me and had always loved me the best she knew how, and my birth father, a new journey in my life.

Despite the sea of people milling around the piazza and the loud and snappy jazz rendition of "Stormy Weather" being played by the bass, piano, and drums on the stage next to me, I saw Tony's dark hair peeking through the crowd and heard him call my name.

"Olivia! Sorry I'm late," he said, dodging in and out of the hordes of people. He sat next to me and leaned in to kiss my cheek. "Where'd everyone come from?"

"About twenty tour buses and two mega cruise ships, actually." I returned his kiss, using my free hand to wave a waiter to our table.

" *Prego?"* asked the waiter.

"Un cappuccino con ciocolatto, per favore," Tony answered, never taking his eyes off mine.

"So, Olivia, what about us?"

"I told you. We'll have to see what happens."

"But I feel so sure. I thought you felt the same way." His brows furrowed, his hand tightening on my arm.

The waiter set Tony's drink on the table.

"It's not that easy. I need to get rid of "stuff" and make that clean final break from my ex. It hasn't even been a year since the divorce was final."

Tony sipped his coffee, the cream and chocolate leaving traces on his upper lip. He licked it clean.

My heart hammered. Every movement he made, his voice, his eyes, everything screamed sensual. Tiny pleasant knots formed in my stomach.

"But you were separated for two years before that."

I breathed in and exhaled slowly, trying to concentrate on our conversation and not on his lips. "It doesn't matter, Tony. I ran. I became a whirling dervish with no direction to avoid facing my pain." I stroked his face, wishing I could just let him rescue me from the hurt. But I couldn't. Not yet.

"But, Olivia…"

Silence.

The jazz trio had upped the tempo with a fast rendition of "New York, New York" throwing the tourists around us into frenzied applause.

A silly man dressed in shorts, T-shirt, white socks and Birkenstocks sandals stood to the side, illegally feeding the pigeons as though trying for a world record for how many he could hold on his body. People twisted from the music to snap photos.

I turned my attention back to Tony. "It has nothing to do with you. It's my mom and Ashley, and my father, Mario, and dealing with a new family, and waiting for my mom to die, and renewing my friendship with a sister. It's so much."

I leaned in to kiss him. He tasted like mocha, the coffee and chocolate perfectly blended on his mouth. "I care about you. I think you're the one man I want to spend the rest of my life with, Tony. But I need to resolve so many things. Then I can concentrate on a marriage. You were talking marriage, weren't you?"

I looked at him, feeling the pull of those espresso eyes.

"Of course, Olivia."

His head fell, and he stared at the ground for a long time. Sighing, he reached over and held my face in his hands and gently kissed me. "You're worth waiting for." He pulled his cell from his shirt pocket, scrolled with his thumb, and said, "Here's what's waiting for you." He pushed the phone towards me. The scene was a crimson sunset over a vineyard on rolling hills. I could see myself standing between the colorful rows of grapes and vines, could feel my feet sinking into the rich soil.

"It's beautiful, Tony. Give me a year. Can you do that? Just one year?"

"You got it, sweetheart. But we'll talk every day and spend weekends together. Now let's talk about this new family of yours. When are they coming to steal you away from me?"

I glanced at my watch. "In about two hours. I asked them for some time after saying goodbye to Mom and Ash. You can join us for dinner if you'd like. It's a loud family, full of love and laughter. I'm still dizzy from yesterday's lunch or '*pranzo*' as they call it. In fact, Ashley enjoyed herself so much she cancelled their flight. My mother slept soundly through lunch despite the chaos. Made it even more difficult to say goodbye this morning." I dug my nails into my hands to keep tears away.

"Dinner sounds great. Although I'd rather be alone with you, I want to meet my future Italian family." He leaned in for a kiss.

He sat back and raised his cup to take another sip. "My flight leaves Marco Polo Airport at seven a.m. tomorrow. And my next few weeks aren't going to be easy."

"I still can't believe you were undercover. Although some things did seem 'off' about you." I paused. "And that Putin-looking guy is, was your handler? Really? He reminded me of a handsome bad guy from a James Bond movie."

"Well, a lot of things were 'off' as you put it. My handler—you call him handsome, I think he looks like a typical East Coast thug–came within inches of sending me back to the States for breaking protocol so many times." His countenance changed from content to concern. "I'm so done with this career. Especially since I found you. It's strange how fast priorities can change. Between meeting you and my phone call to Vince, I knew immediately I had to redirect my future."

"I'm happy for you, Tony."

"Finish that coffee, Olivia. Let's get lost in the alleys."

He took my hand, and we shouldered our way through the piazza to one of the many narrow alleys darting from the main square. We strolled, hand in hand, enjoying the window displays. One window was full paintings by local artists, and a souvenir shop caught my eye. We walked into the store, and I purchased some Burano glass necklaces for friends. The aroma of fresh pizza drifted from a restaurant, tempting us to taste. Contentment. There wasn't anything like it. Contentment mixed with incredible sparks of romance.

Tony stopped suddenly, took me by the shoulders, leaned me onto an ancient wall in the alley and kissed me with such passion, I swore the earth moved. My knees weak, my breath ragged, I whispered his name.

Rubbing his thumb over my lips, he asked, "Still want to wait a year, *cara mia?*"

"Since you put it that way," I said, "maybe not.

The End

Book Club Questions:

*I*t has often been said we are the product of our environment. How does being adopted confirm this? Or does it?

Having a verbally abusive father can color everything in a young girl's life. How did this affect Ashley? How did it affect you if you experienced it?

How would Olivia's view of life been different if her real father had been revealed at a younger age, or in a different way?

How does alcoholism affect family dynamics?

Finding your family's roots is difficult at best. How do you suppose Olivia was able to find her birth father? Would you have been driven to do the same thing?

How involved have you ever been with total strangers you've met on a cruise? Has it stirred your compassion, curiosity, disdain, etc.?

Being introduced to new places via a cruise, how would it change your world view? Do new places excite you?

What propelled Veronica to turn to alcohol? And what could have been done to help her. How did this affect both Ashley and Olivia?

Do you believe forgiveness is the best way to heal family relationships?

Does forgiveness mean you must be a part of this dysfunctional person's life?

Why do you think Tony was so attracted to Olivia?

How long do you think it takes to "recover" from a divorce?

Have present day events made travel less attractive? Or do you want to explore no matter the circumstances? Why or why not?

What makes people go into any kind of secret service organization, either government or private? What toll does it take on the person's life?

Do you think Tony will be able to escape the grip of NeroMare?

How do you think Ashley and Olivia will grieve for their mother?

How difficult would it be for a family to accept such a surprising discovery of a "secret" child? What would you do? Would you welcome the intrusion and be generous in the welcome. Would you be angry?

How do you think each character will deal with their new reality?

How will you end the story? Will Olivia and Tony marry? I think they will!

Acknowledgements

There are so many people who have helped me with this novel. I must give special thanks to my loyal critique group: Dennis Phinney, a brilliant and descriptive writer of historical fiction; Brenda Barrie, with several novels under her belt and with many quick fixes to my work; John C. Gray, a word craftsman extraordinaire with whom I am co-authoring a romance novel (set in Italy, of course); Ana Arellano, the young writer to watch who will be working on her graduate degree in Ireland; MJ Buist, who keeps me grounded with reality; Dr. Ed Kaufman, the psychiatrist who lets me know if I'm hitting the right emotional notes on my characters; and Herb Williams-Dalgart, whose edits amaze me with his clarity and teaches me to trust my words….all experienced writers and authors.

In addition, thanks to my wonderful readers: David Spiselman, Catherine Drake, and Nancy Thorne.

And to my dear friend, Dr. Jim Hills, who edited the book and spent hours critiquing and making important changes.

I also want to acknowledge the Orange County Chapter of the California Writer's Club for the invaluable speakers, mentors, and authors who share their experience and knowledge at each meeting.

About the Author

*J*anet Simcic is a free-lance writer from Southern California. Her articles have appeared in many magazines as well as the Orange County Register. Her first novel, _The Man at the Caffe' Farnese_ will have a sequel in 2015....*The Man at the Spanish Steps*. This novel is one of four in the "The Man at...." series.

Her extensive travel to Italy, her love of the culture and language, prompted her to write a non-fiction book...*An American Chick's Guide to Italy*.

She enjoys writing, traveling, polishing her fluency with the Italian language, and consulting with travelers who are going to Italy for the first time.

Janet is active in the California Writers Club, community activities, her church, directs a critique group and loves spending time with her 14 grandchildren. She is an avid reader. Her top favorite authors are Nicholas Sparks, Daniel Silva, and Brad Thor.

Website: www.janetsimcic.com